THINKING SIDEWAYS

Short Stories Both Real and Imaginary

DONALD E. SMITH, PH.D

authorHOUSE®

AuthorHouse™
1663 Liberty Drive
Bloomington, IN 47403
www.authorhouse.com
Phone: 1 (800) 839-8640

Published by AuthorHouse 10/15/2015

ISBN: 978-1-5049-5688-8 (sc)
ISBN: 978-1-5049-5687-1 (e)

Library of Congress Control Number: 2015917236

Print information available on the last page.

CONTENTS

FOREWORD

This is my first attempt at writing short stories. I've been told that it might be the most difficult of genres. The entire premise of what one wants to relate must be compressed into something brief enough to be classified as being "short." Plot and characters must be developed without excessive or flowery prose.

It's, also, my first attempt at fiction. Five of my other six books were non-fiction and the other one was poetry. I call the following stories fiction, but, in reality, they are a mixture of both fact and fiction. Some are purely fiction. And, some are mostly fact with an embellishment of fiction added for texture. It's incumbent upon the reader to determine which one is which. It shouldn't matter.

Some stories are based loosely upon my career in education. Some are based upon those random slices of the lives that all of us experience. A third group defies catagorization.

The stories were derived from my eighty-five years of living. Some characters are real, some are imaginary and some are a synthesis of more than one person. It doesn't really matter. They existed in some form, either in real life or in my mind. The question that is asked often is: "What is reality?" The lines between reality and fantasy become blurred easily. Often, our imaginary lives become more important to us than what we do in our mundane daily living. When we were young, imagination played a big role. At the end of life, it resumes that same importance. In these stories, I've tried to point out some common human virtues and some common frailties, the things that we all have in varying amounts. I hope that the stories lend voice to the many things that we leave unspoken, but care about deeply.

I hope that they touch a heart string or dredge up some memories. Open your minds to the endless possibilities that just the act of living gives to all of us. If you haven't performed the actions and haven't felt the emotions of those who inhabit these stories, know that you can experience the entire gamut and range of human experience vicariously through the act of reading. Free yourselves from the restraints that time, age and frailty impose upon all of us. Let your imaginations soar. If some of the characters and their actions seem implausable, heed the words of the Roman poet, Terrance, who said: "Nothing human is strange or alien to me."

ACKNOWLEDGEMENTS

I didn't write these stories in a vacuum. I need to acknowledge the people who have helped to shape my life and who played important roles in the writing of this book.

First and foremost, are my family, both past and present. Next, come my friends, classmates and the colleagues from my various jobs.

Another big role was played by those whom I met while traveling or teaching overseas in the fifty-two countries that I've been fortunate to have visited. They added a flavor, a fillip, to the heady stew of characters who populated my life.

A special thanks goes to Roger Stevenson who harnessed my excessive verbosity and made me see the value of clarity and minimalism. He was ruthless in coaching me to say only what was essential to further the stories. Thanks, also, to Mark Lawver who read some of the stories and offered honest advice and opinions. I didn't show the stories to family members except for a few brief glimpses. I wanted to surprise them.

All of those people and many more whom I could mention, helped to shape and mold me into what I am today. We are intertwined forever. I am them and they are me. Together, we form the the entity that the world knows as Donald Smith.

I dedicate this book to all of those whose lives have rubbed against mine. It's the friction from that intentional and unintentional rubbing that created the warmth and the spark of energy that enabled me to write this book. I hope that the book creates a spark in you.

A HARROWING EXPERIENCE

I took the tube's blue line from Heathrow to the Earl's Court station. From there, I changed to the green line to Paddington Station where I switched to the maroon Line to Harrow-on-the Hill. I had taken an over-night flight from JFK to Heathrow. I was tired and a little irritable. I had thought that Richard would meet me at Heathrow and drive me to his home in this quaint, ancient town in the hills just north of London. But, he had written to me before my departure and said that he would be too busy on the day of my arrival to meet me. He said that it would be easy for me to use the tube to reach his home from the airport.

Really? Well, easy it wasn't. I had to carry my large suitcase, my carry-on and my camera bag all the way. When Richard visited me in Ohio, I had met him at Hopkins Airport in Cleveland. I made a 100-mile round trip from my home near Akron to make things easy for Richard.

So, yes, I was tired and irritable. The little town of Harrow-on-the Hill was story-book cute. I had read about its history and its famous boys' boarding school. Even the tube station was cute. But, I wasn't in the mood for cute. I wanted to get to Richard's house, take a shower and have a nap. I'd been up for almost two days. Richard had said that his home was just a few blocks from the station. But, the few blocks turned into, by my count, eight and half blocks of sturdy stone structures and Tudor-style homes.

With my fully loaded suitcase in my right hand, my carry-on in my left hand and my heavy camera bag over my shoulder, I trudged along while grumbling to myself and sweating profusely. I cursed at Richard under my breath, berating him for being so selfish and inconsiderate. I had treated him with respect and generosity during his week-long stay at my home. Now, this is what I get in return.

Richard and I belonged to a secondary school administrators' exchange program. Members were to visit each other's schools and take an active role in the day-to-day duties of being a principal. My serving as a host during the previous school year had been, I had thought, very successful. I had looked forward to visiting Richard on his home turf. And, now, this. I stopped periodically to rest my weary arms and back. He'd better have something for me to eat and drink and a place to lie down.

I took another look at the directions that Richard had sent me. It looked like his house just down this street on the left. It was a small brick house with white-painted wooden areas to give it a pseudo-Tudor appearance. I walked up to the door and knocked. And, knocked. No one answered my first five knocks. The windows were covered with heavy drapes and no sounds came from inside.

Now, I was really pissed! After all of this, why was there no one at home to meet me?

Then, the door opened just a crack and I saw two pairs of eyes looking at me with skepticism. One pair was far above my head and the other pair was far below my head. Was I at the right house? I asked, "Is Richard home?" No answer. Just the two sets of eyes staring at me from the crack of the partially opened door. I said to the eyes, "My name is Don. Richard is expecting me." The door opened just a little wider. I could see that it wasn't Richard and a dog, but a tall man and a small woman.

I asked, "Is Richard here?" Again, silence. But, the door opened wider and the tall man motioned for me to come in. The little lady looked down at the floor and flashed a demure smile. I hesitated. Should I go in? Is this Richard's home? Who are these people? The man handed me a note. It said, "Don, I'm sorry, but I'm tied up with an important school meeting. My boarders will get you settled in."

Okay, then. I followed the disparate pair into a back bedroom. The man motioned for me to put down my luggage. The little lady smiled again. Neither one had uttered a word. The man looked to be Indian. He wore a turban and had a mustache and goatee. The lady just seemed depressed. Richard had not mentioned that he had boarders. The man closed my bedroom door behind them as they left. The room had a double bed, a vanity, a rocking chair and a clothes rack. I lay down on the bed and closed my eyes. I resolved to investigate the odd couple later.

For now, I'll just rest a few minutes. Two hours later, I awoke. Richard's face was looking down on me. "Welcome to Harrow-on-the-Hill, Don. I hope you've had a nice trip." I said to myself, "No thanks to you, you inconsiderate bugger."

A little later, over cups of coffee, I complained to Richard about his lack of courtesy and consideration. He just smiled and said that he knew that I could navigate from Heathrow to his home with no problem. I told him to stick his explanation up his scrawny English bum. He responded that we Americans often substituted crude comments for proper English language. We knew each oher well enough to not take offense.

I asked him about the two who had met me at the door. He said that the tall Indian was a deaf mute who was attending a special school for those afflicted in that way. With government support, he was learning to use sign language and to lip-read. The government paid for his room and board with Richard. He was seven feet tall; eight, counting the turban.

The quiet little lady had been released recently from a mental hospital. She suffered from severe depression due to the loss of her husband and two small children in a tragic automobile accident. The government paid Richard for her room and board, also. She would live here until the doctors decided that she could live on her own. So, there we were. An acerbic, divorced, sarcastic British educator, the Indian mute, a devastated little lady and me, the hungry, sleepy, angry American who wished that he had never come.

I looked down at my coffee. I asked Richard why we were drinking coffee and not tea as I had imagined all proper Englishmen did, especially in mid-afternoon. Richard just smiled. I hated that sneer of a smile. But, that was Richard. Ever sarcastic, ever inscrutable. When our cups were empty and put aside, the little lady scurried in and took them into the kitchen. The tall Indian just stood close and looked down on us.

That night, we watched some telly. The BBC featured English programs, of course. I had always enjoyed those same programs back home. The four of us sat in almost complete silence. Richard was taciturn as usual. The turbinator couldn't talk. The little lady chose not to talk. I was too tired to talk. At ten o'clock, I announced that I was ready for bed. I used the loo before entering my bedroom. As soon as I left the loo, the little lady entered it, mopped the floor and swabbed out the toilet. That was her standard practice throughout my stay.

When I turned down my bed covers, I saw that an electric heating pad had been placed on top of the bottom sheet. The English nights tend to be cold and the house had no central heating system, just an electric heater in each room. The heating pad was a nice touch. I climbed into bed, perchance to sleep. The bedroom door opened just a crack and three sets of eyes peered at me from various heights. I peered back before the door closed silently.

I didn't wake up until ten the next morning. Richard had already left for school. The two boarders were sitting in the small dining area drinking coffee. I told them that I would like to take a bath. I hadn't had one for almost three days.

The little lady arose from her chair, scurried to the small bathroom and began to draw water for my bath. I took my clothes for the day into the bathroom, took off my boxer shorts and tee shirt and lowered myself into the steaming water. But, the room was cold, English cold. Two sets of eyes appeared in the crack of the partially open door. As if I had announced my being cold, the little lady entered the room and plugged in the electric heater. Richard had told me the night before that the hot water was only available twice each day, morning and night, for a period of about an hour. Saving money, you know.

I had noticed that the loo, the toilet, was in a separate small room, not in the bathroom. The English, as most Europeans, like to separate their body functions as much as possible. Good idea, I thought.

After my bath, I dressed in my blue sport jacket, grey slacks and white shirt with a blue and red striped tie. Richard had said that the high school was a short walk from his house. As with many things, Richard's idea of a short walk was different from mine.

As I prepared to leave, I heard sounds emanating from Richard's bedroom. Then an attractive young lady came out of the bedroom. She said, "You must be Don. Richard has talked a lot about you. I'm Sarah, his girl friend."

Well, I thought, this little house is just full of surprises. I knew that Richard had been divorced recently and that his children lived with their mother. But, he hadn't mentioned his live-in girl friend. She looked to be quite a bit younger than Richard.

After a few minutes of chit-chat, I started on my walk to the high school following Richard's hurriedly spoken directions. The "Short walk" turned out to be a thirty minute trek. I passed through blocks of brick and stone houses. I went by several parks filled with ancient trees and well-tended flower gardens. As it was still early in the morning, I saw only a few people. Those whom I saw, waved and mouthed English accented "Good mornings."

When I arrived at the two story brick high school, I was a little tired and more than a little sweaty even though the air was brisk. The school was tucked neatly into a crowded residential area. It was what we would call a public school. It was not the famous Harrow school for boys or either of two religious schools that served the towns of Harrow and Harrow-on-the Hill.

I saw some students in the paved area behind the school wearing their red and white uniforms. To my surprise, most of the students were black. later, I would learn that the town had a large black population, most of whom came from former British colonial possessions.. Some boys were playing basketball. I asked one of the boys where the principal's office was located. He looked at me with quizically. He said, "Principal?" I remembered that Richard was the headmaster, not the principal. I asked him where the headmaster's office was. The boy's eyes lit up and he said in a crisp British accent, "Follow me, sir."

I entered Richard's second floor office. Of course, he wasn't there. His secretary said he'd gone to the nearby elementary school to talk to its headmaster about neighborhood problems. She said that Richard had arranged for me to use his office for the day as he wouldn't be back until later in the afternoon. I entered the small, but cozy office. It looked like any other school administrator's office with one big exception. It had a well-stocked liquor cabinet. The secretary saw me staring at the cabinet. She said, "Richard invites selected senior students to meet with him each day for lunch and a glass of sherrry.. "Oh," I said, "How British!" I wondered if I could introduce this civilized custom back home. Yeah, right!

I spent the day roaming about the building, popping in and out of classrooms to the consternation of surprised teachers. Apparently, Richard hadn't told them of my visit. Of course, he hadn't.

I went out onto the couryard from time to time and talked to students who were permitted to be outside during their "Break period." I admired their well-ironed combinations of red and white dresses, trousers, sweaters, shirts and jackets. Their shiny dark faces contrasted well against the bright colors. I laughed inwardly at their pronounced British accents. To me, their accents seemed incongruous with their ethnicity. I noticed one frail blonde girl sitting in a remote corner of the courtyard. I walked over and saw that she had been crying. "Can I help?" I asked. "No, sir, no one can." She told me that she was bullied every day by the black girls. I told her that I'd talk to the headmaster about her problem when he returned. She said that he hadn't been able to stop the bullying and that her parents planned to move to another school district if they could find affordable lodging here. How familiar that sounded. I would, still, try to help her during my time at the school.

The day passed quickly. Richard had not returned to the school. I began the "short" walk back to his house. When I arrived, Richard was sitting in the kitchen with his cup of coffee. "How did your day go, Don?" I just looked at him. Was this a test of my patience? I went to my room and changed into more comfortable clothing. I planned to challenge him as to his strange behavior. When I went back into the kitchen, he was gone. The two boarders were at the table with their coffees. I asked slowly and distinctly, "Where is Richard?" They both pointed to his bedroom and grinned their first grins. The Indian held up two fingers. I got the message. The girl friend had returned as well.

The days followed in a predictable manner. I visited the high school daily. I spoke to the assembled students in the middle and elementary schools. I talked about America and answered their questions. I tried to correct the many misconceptions that they had about the culture in the United States. "No, I don't know any cowboys or gangsters. I don't own a gun. I've never killed any one. I am not wealthy." Most of the false impressions, I realized, had come from watching our American tv shows and movies.

I talked to the combined faculties of all three schools. I led a discussion that compared the educational systems in our two countries. Oh, and I continued Richard's custom of drinking sherry with the senior students at the high school.

But, Richard was not around very much. He dropped in to the high school for an hour or so each day. He usually left the house each morning before I got up and came back home after I'd gone to bed. My evenings were spent sitting on the sofa with the Indian the the depressed lady watching telly. We didn't talk. Obviously. Richard did say that I should go into London on the tube and do some sightseeing. He said the little lady would go with me to show me how to navigate the tube system.

One Saturday, I took him up on his suggestion. The lady and I rode in silence. We looked at the sights in silence and we ate fish and chips in silence. It was an exhilarating experience.

I began to wonder more about Richard. I tried to question his girl friend about his strange demeanor. But, she clammed up quickly. Now, I had to contend with three silent people and one person who was hardly ever present. I wondered why had come here. I thought I had come to learn about the English educational system. What I found were four people who had chosen to ignore me. Richard had been outgoing and vocal when he visited with me in the United States. In America, he was lively, funny and very involved. He wanted to learn and experience all that he could. Now, he was secretive and unavailable. I thought about returning home ahead of schedule.

One morning, I arose to use the loo and I overheard Richard talking on the phone. He sounded agitated and a little angry. I heard comments such as, "This was bad timing. We shouldn't have started this until after Don left." "I can't afford to lose this money. I worry that those two will lose their cover and blow up the whole operation."

Wow, I thought, what has Richard gotten himself into? All kinds of wild scenarios crossed and recrossed my mind. Was Richard in trouble? Were criminal elements involved? Was I at risk or in danger? I needed to find out more. Maybe, I should just pack up and leave. Were the Indian and the little lady complicit in whatever it was? Was the girl friend involved, also? My inquiring mind wanted to know more. I couldn't just leave without knowing.

I channeled Sherlock Holmes. The ambiance was right for sleuthing. What better place to solve a mystery than in the storied town of Harrow in the misty hills high above Old London Town.

I decided to listen more closely and snoop more professionally. That night, after I had retired, I got up silently, opened my door slightly and listened to a very quiet conversation between the Indian and the little lady. They sat on the sofa knee to knee in deep intimate discourse. I couldn't make out the words. But, they were talking. That, in itself, was a shock. Supposedly, the Indian couldn't talk and the lady was too depressed to talk. But, talk they did. As I watched, Richard and his girl friend opened their bedroom door and joined the hushed discussion. They seemed concerned and, even, afraid. I began to formulate a theory. But, it was only a theory yet to be tested. I closed the door and lay down on my bed with ideas swarming about in my mind. I hoped that my theory would not turn out to be true.

I missed the old Richard, caustic, annoying, but fun and entertaining. The next evening, I tried to loosen him up and release my old friend and colleague. I, even, tried a few lame jokes. Jokes with sexual innuendos had always worked with him. I asked him what the true definition of an English gentleman was. He just looked at me with a hint of annoyance lurking behind his dark, piercing eyes. I said, "A true English gentleman puts most of his weight on his elbows." He tried not to laugh, but a little one sneaked out. I followed this with, "What does an English mother say to her daughter just before she is to be married? She says, "Just lie back and think of England." Richard just nodded and arose to leave the room. I called after him, "What the hell is wrong with you?" He turned with a scowl and said, "You're what's wrong with me. I wish that you had stayed home." He went into his bedroom and slammed the door. Well, I thought, that went well.

I decided to work on the boarders and, maybe, the girl friend. I could confront them or I could try to trick them into revealing what was going on. I had, already, thought of a few ways to approach them. Of course, I could just return to my home earlier than I planned and leave this motley crew to their fate. But, I decided to give it a good old college try before I left the scene of the, uh, crime. I hoped that what ever it was, was not a crime.

That night, I heard the usual sounds of amore coming through the thin walls from the next room, But, I also heard more subdued discussion coming from the living room. Again, I cracked open my door and listened. The Indian and the little lady were joined eventually by Richard and his girl friend. I heard Richard say, "Don seems to be getting a little suspicious. We need to be careful around him. Just a few more weeks and we'll have earned enough money to give up this whole business. Don't blow it now!"

It was curiouser and curiouser. If those are real words. Am I being complicit in whatever they are doing? Could I be detained in England as a material witness? Should I just go home now? Nah! Inquiring minds need to know.

The next morning, I looked at the Indian and asked him point-blank, "Can you talk? Can you hear?" He looked at me with wide eyes and turned away.

When the little lady began to clear away my breakfast dishes, I asked her bluntly, "Were your husband and children killed in an automobile accident? Have you been diagnosed with severe depression?" She looked at me and walked away slowly.

As I arose from the table, I noticed that the girl friend had been listening. She walked quickly to the front door, hurried out and walked briskly down the street.

Well, Mr. Don Detective, your direct approach to investigation didn't work, did it?

I decided just to keep my ears and eyes open as I followed what had become a routine. I spent most of the day at the high school. I made short visits to the middle and elementary schools. I was gaining a good perspective on the British educational system. The students seemed more advanced than our students of the same ages. But, that was a generalization, I knew. I met with parent groups from all three schools in the evenings. I enjoyed the discussions about our differences and similarities.

Richard hung around long enough to ask if I were content with what I was doing and inquired if I had any suggestions about what else I might be doing. He suggested that I could visit his divorced sister who lived nearby if I needed more socialization. That was an interesting idea, but I declined demurely. I didn't need any more intrigue. It made me wonder if he were setting me up for a liaison which he would use as leverage to me quiet if I uncovered their secrets. You know - blackmail.

The days passed swiftly. In a few days, I would be heading for Heathrow and home. Richard still stayed away, doing something somewhere. The Indian and the little lady hovered around watching my every move. The girlfriend came and went quickly and silently. The high school students had accepted me as both a quasi headmaster and a curiosity. The senior students and I continued to enjoy our noon-time beverages. I was almost resigned to never knowing what going on. Almost.

When I approached Richard's home after school hours on the day before I was to leave for Heathrow, I sensed that something had either happened or was about to happen. Two large black cars were parked on the street in front of the house. The front door, which had always been closed, was standing wide open. I heard loud, agitated voices coming from inside. The little lady emerged, sat down on the front steps and began to sob. The Indian soon followed, stooping to avoid hitting his head on the door frame.

I paused, not wanting to intrude on whatever was transpiring. As I watched, the girl friend came out with her hands behind her back escorted by a female bobby. Then, Richard appeared, hands behind his back and two burly male bobbies on each side. He noticed me and flashed his sardonic smile. I walked up closer and asked, "Can I help in any way?" He said, "You'll find out soon enough. It will make for a good story for you when you get back home. As for helping, you've done quite enough, already, thank you very much." With that, the four of them were shoved into the two large black cars. Away they went down the quaint streets of Old Harrow Town. The sight and sounds of the cars diminished with distance. I was left alone in the pseudo-Tudor home on Mulberry Street.

What to do next? Should I just pack up and head for home? Maybe, a neighbor would know something. But, I'd never met any neighbors except for one old lady who lived next door. There were no front porches on which to chat. The English were notoriously private and spurned any attempts to pry into their personal affairs. But, I wouldn't be satisfied until I knew *something*.

I remembered seeing Richard stop to talk to the old lady next door. He had mentioned to me that Widow Smethers knew everything that went on in the neighborhood. She had nothing better to do than make it her business to be the eyes and ears of her patch of the neighborhood. It would be worth a try.

I knocked on the widow's door. I saw her peering out from the peep hole. She opened the door cautiously. "Aren't you the American staying with Richard?" "Yes," I answered, "I am. May I ask you a question?"

"Come in, come in. Take a seat. It's not often I get to talk to Americans. What is it that you want to know?" I entered the parlor and sat down on a large overstuffed chair. "May I get you something to drink?" she asked. "Some tea would be nice. All I've gotten at Richards' was coffee," I answered. Smiling, she went to her kitchen and returned soon with a full tea service on a polished silver platter.

"Now, what is it you want to know?" Everything I thought, but I'll just ask her about today's events and what led up to them.

"Do you know why Richard and his friends were taken away by the police?" She thought a moment, sized me up for another long moment, and began to tell me all that she knew about the situation. She, obviously, was proud of her knowledge and pleased to have a receptive audience. This moment was what she lived for. Her watchfulness and abiliity to put two and two together were paying off. She was happy to prove that even though her eyesight was failing and her hearing was poor, her perception of what people were up to was still good.

I listened intently to her long, almost non-stop monologue. It seemed to be cathartic for her to be able to tell all that she had learned after months of watching and listening. She knew that many neighbors thought of her as being just a senile busybody who snooped and pried about into their daily and nightly activities. Telling this story would validate her vigilance and perserverance.

And so the tale unfolded. I listened with fascination, knowing that not everything she said would be the exact truth. I knew that I would have to separate fact from fantasy and conjecture. But, an eyewitness is like gold in this sleuthing business.

She had met the Indian, Sachman Samrath, in the local fish and chips establishment. He had bumped into her accidently and had apologized profusely. In their brief conversation, he had said that he was moving into the neighborhood with his wife, Molly. As he talked, it became clear that he and Molly were moving into Richard's house which was next door to her. Sachman steered her over to where his wife was waiting for her fish and chips. His wife was a quiet little Caucasian woman. Mrs. Smethers left, knowing that they would be seeing each other very soon.

Some days later, she ran into Constable Simmons at the grocer's. He was an old school chum of hers. After some friendly chit-chat, he asked her if she'd met the headmaster's new boarders. She told him of her meeting them at the fish and chips shoppe. She said that they'd had a nice talk and that she'd been looking forward to talking to them again.

In the days that followed, she observed that the two new neighbors seldom left Richard's house. When she saw of them outside, she would call a "Hello" or a "Cheerio" to them. They never responded verbally. They either ignored her or waved. She had thought their behavior was strange, especially after the pleasant exchange in the fish shoppe. But, "You know how people are these days. It's an unsettling time that we live in."

I continued to listen intently, not quite knowing where the old lady's story would take me. She moved closer and continued in a more subdued voice. She glanced around as if to make certain that no one else was listening. Was this to be only unsubstantiated gossip? She leaned even closer and in a whisper said, "Do you know what I found out?" No, I didn't. Just get on with it you old biddy.

"Well, I did some snooping around. I talked to my friend, Mr. Smythe, who is high up in the local authority. He told me that Richard was receiving monies from the local authority for housing a deaf mute and a former mental patient. Can you believe it? I saw and heard wih my own eyes and ears that both of them are perfecly normal. At least, as normal as those Indian chaps can be. I'd put nothing past some of those foreigners. And, that wife of his ! Tsk! No self-respecting English woman would marry out of her race."

She looked at me with a proud smile. She knew that this was a juicy bit. "And, to top it off, my other friend told me that Richard had fallen behind in his mortgage payment and was at risk of losing his house. Can you believe it? Him, in his high and mighty job as a headmaster. It just goes to show that a hoity-toity education doesn't make you all that."

Well, this last bit of information was a shocker. Richard and his motley crew were involved in scamming the local government. My arrival had made it very difficult for them to keep up the charade. I remembered that

I had written to Richard some time ago and said that I needed to begin my stay with him some five weeks earlier than I had planned originally. Alas, poor Richard! I thought I knew him well.

Before I leave for home, I should say goodbye to Richard if I can find him.. He's, probably, in one of those "Gated" communities (aka jail). I know he'll be glad to see me. I can't say that I'll miss the tall Indian and the little woman, but his girl friend was cute. I never did get to meet his sister. It's just as well. I will miss the students, especially, the seniors who shared Richard's sherry with me.

As for me helping to cause Richards' problems, I didn't feel guilty. It was old Mrs. Smether's who ratted him out.. Even though I'd offered, there really wasn't anything I could do to help him. As Richard said before getting into the police car, "It will make a good story for you when you get back home."

I am telling the story now to pay him back for not meeting me at Heathrow as any proper Englishman should have done. But, I'd never thought of Richard as proper.

WHEN THE LAUGHTER STOPPED

Mr. Melhorne didn't like teaching. He never did. But, what else could he have done? He was a klutz. A genuine and pathetic klutz.

He was good at collecting facts and good at telling people about those facts. He loved facts. So, he became a teacher in order to stay in his comfort zone. Three decades of students had suffered through his boring lectures and monologues. He reeked of banalities. His students and his colleagues laughed at him and at his clumsy efforts to be relevant.

He was never bad enough to be fired and just good enough to be kept on.

His close-cut hair, white dress shirts, slim black ties, pointy black shoes and Mr. Rogers cardigans were truth-in-packaging. He looked like what he was - a bona-fide klutz.

He addressed the boys as "Young sirs." He called the girls "Young ladies." He never understood the teen-age banter which swirled about him like smog. The music that emanated from countless cell phones and I-Pads confused and irritated him. He didn't understand his students and they didn't care to try to understand him.

But, he survived by just doing his job. No more, no less. He arrived at school at exactly the same time each day. Early. He stayed late in his classroom, head down, grading papers and planning lessons for the next day. He graded papers quickly and wrote terse comments in red ink along the margins He used few adjectives or adverbs. He dealt in absolutes. He was no-nonsense.

He seldom praised or censored. His language was pure vanilla. Exotic flavors made him nervous and gave him headaches.

When he finished with his work, he hurried down the empty hallways hoping to avoid all other human life. He looked around the parking lot to be certain that no one was lurking about, opened his car door with the remote while still several yards away and jumped in quickly. The 1992 Chevy Cavalier was filled with the detritus of his well-planned miserable life.

He drove slowly and carefully to his rented rooms in a big, old home in the once-fashionable part of town. He had a small sitting room, a bedroom and a tiny bathroom. Lion head claws supported the big bathtub. He longed for a shower, but made do with a sit down bath and a long rubber hose which had a shower head on it.

He shared a kitchen with three other renters. He ate sparsely so that his kitchen-time was barely noticeable to the other tenants.

Every night, Mr. Melhorne lay down on his army-style cot and re-played the day in his mind. Nothing stood out. Nothing ever did. He stared at the water stained ceiling for a while. He decided to turn on the black and white nineteen inch television to provide some background noise to cover his sobbing. Sobbing was what he did each day upon returning to his rooms. It was the only emotion that he permitted for himself. He used it to clear his head from the terrible thoughts that, somehow, would creep in at an ever increasing rate.

Melhorne had no contact with students or teachers outside of school hours. He liked it that way. He avoided his housemates as much as possible. He didn't know their names. He never asked. He knew that they thought him odd. He couldn't disagree.

He never attended any school functions or athletic events. He never volunteered for anything. When students were asked about their teachers from prior years, his name never came up.

He taught and lived under the table and off the grid. He was a black-market man through and through.

If he had a life outside of school hours, (and he did not), no one knew or cared. He stayed in his classroom during his free periods with his head buried in his hands. To anyone peering through the window in his classroom door, he appeared to be deep in thought or taking a sit-up nap.

The faculty lounge never knew his presence. At lunchtime, he ate his cheese sandwich on white bread and drank his half-pint of white milk alone in his room. He never used condiments or ate dessert.

When asked how he was doing he responded with a polite, "Fine, thanks, thanks for asking."

When invited to any function, he told them that he couldn't make it, but "Thanks for asking."

He was a mystery that no one cared to solve. He was part of the school community, but not connected to it by any kind of human thread. He was odd and eccentric, but he gave the others someone to measure themselves against. They all felt better about themselves by comparison.

The administration and the school board knew he was odd. They prided themselves for keeping him. It gave the school a kind of ..... diversity. He was an odd duck, but he was their odd duck.

Parents never complained about Mr. Melhorne because their children never mentioned his name. He lived in anonymity. He wanted it that way.

So, it was a big surprise and a huge shock when he arrived at school one brisk November Friday wearing only a thong, hunting boots and a superman cape flowing about his scrawny shoulders. His newly shaved head gleamed brightly in the morning light which streamed through the lobby windows. He greeted the amazed students and staff who were mingling about with a loud "Hello". He had never spoken that loudly before. Shocked and even frightened, the assemblage laughed nervously at what they hoped would be a kind of sick joke. But, although few knew him, they all knew that Mr. Melhorne never joked.

He carried a guitar case covered with travel stickers from places he'd never been. He placed the case on the floor. He flashed a big smile and announced in a lilting sing-song voice, "My name is Ed, Ed Melhorne. I don't know any of you by name, nor do I care to. But, I do know that after today, you will all know me. You will remember me to your dying day."

He opened the case and did what he'd come there to do.

The nervous laughter soon stopped.

THEY NEVER CALLED
HIM MISTER

Harold worked in the bowels of the school. He toiled among the hot boilers, dirty coal and sweaty pipes. Unlike those who worked above him, he used his hands, legs and back. Oh, he had a brain, but it seldom had a real work-out. He did things by rote memory. He had forgotten his dream of going to college and wearing a suit and tie to work. Instead, he wore the same pair of bib overalls for a week before giving them to his wife to wash.

He considered the stains and smudges to be stigmatae, his penitence for allowing life to deprive him of his dreams. For that reason and many others, he hated life. He hated his life in particular.

He grew more and more sensitive to what people called him. He was called a janitor, a custodian, a maintenence man. He was the guy who came to clean up messes when he was called over the intercom. The principal called him Harold. Most teachers didn't know his first name. They just rang him up and said, "Someone just threw up. Come to my room and clean it up." The kids made up stories about what was below the first floor. They had heard from older students that strange noises, strange happenings went on down there. Harold's domain was off-limits to students. Teachers weren't the least bit curious. They would not want to dirty their clothes or their skin down there to find out.

The worst thing for Harold was that no one called him Mr. Bolton. He would have loved to have been called "Mr." just once.

Harold did his work well. He was granted annual raises based on both longevity and merit. There never was any thought of replacing him. Many times, he wished he would be replaced. Maybe, that would have impelled him to find a better job or to take college courses in the evenings. But, family obligations, the mortgage, the car payments, hungry kids and a wife who preferred the status quo, dulled his ambition. He grew more satisfied, if not happy. His life as Harold, the fixer-upper and the mopper-upper went on in soul-destroying monotony.

It wasn't until "Hey you" was used more frequently than his other names that he snapped out of his doldrums. "Hey you" was just not acceptable. He deserved better than that. Maybe, he thought, if I change my appearance, I'll get more respect. Maybe, they'll even call me "Mister."

So it was, that one fine warm April day, Harold came to work, not in his bib overalls, but in a spiffy black, pin-striped suit complete with cuffed white shirt and red silk tie. He arrived early as usual and went down into the bowels of the building. He was careful not to touch anything that would mark him with dirt or grease. He sat at his battered old desk and waited for someone to call him on the inter-com. At 9:30, a call came in. Mrs. Morgan's shrill demanding voice said, "This is room 231. Get up here right away. One of my students vomited all over his desk and on the floor. I need you to mop it up and disinfect everything. And, hurry up!"

Harold smiled a rare smile, grabbed his pail, mop and bottle of Clorox and left his domain. He exited the service elevator near to room 231 and marched in proudly in his spotless attire. Mrs. Morgan looked at him in surprise and stifled a smirk. The kids laughed out loud. They had never seen Harold, the fixer-upper and mopper-upper look like this.

Harold did his duty and hurried back to his safe-place. He was embarrassed and ashamed. He had hoped that his new look would gain him respect. Instead, it had only made them laugh.

He tried to concentrate on his daily routine. He realized that the old boilers needed more coal. He went to the coal bin, shoveled some coal on the conveyor and waited until he could load more coal on it. He leaned over to lay more coal on the moving belt and felt a sharp tug on his neck. His new, shiny red silk tie had been caught in the mechanism. He was pulled into the open maw of the furnace, kicking and screaming all of the way.

Mrs. Morgan heard the screams through the inter-com. Harold had forgotten to shut it off. She shouted "Harold," "Harold," "Mr. Bolton!" They were the last words that he ever heard.

TOKE-BOY

That new stuff I'd bought was really good. I felt warm and comfortable. My mind was in a good place. Cares, worries? I had none.

I smiled at Mom and gave her a big hug. "See you later Momio. I might be a little late if I stop at Billy's."

Mom was a trusting soul. She never doubted my words or my actions. She thought that my mellow attitude was a result of good parenting and plenty of love.

When I arrived at school, I ducked into the first floor boys' bathroom for a quick puff or two. Luckily, the room was empty. I needed the confidence that weed gave me. In spite of my outward show of bravado and machismo, I lived in perpetual doubt and fear.

I had only average grades. I was not an athlete. I couldn't sing well or play an instrument. My persona was one of someone who took chances. Someone who lived on the edge. I knew where to score the stuff. I was a source of knowledge about the world of drugs and how to fool your family and the school. For those reasons, I was accepted by those who aspired to be like me.

I left the bathroom ready to meet the daily challenges. For it was a challenge to pretend that I was just a normal, very average student at Highpoint High. I felt far better than average. I was smarter and far more clever than those suck-up honor roll students or those posturing letter winners. I was a super hero. I could save the world. I could fly, even soar. I could ace today's history test even though I'd never read a word of the chapter on which we'd be tested. I could do thirty push-ups in today's gym class without breaking a sweat.

I could get a date with any of those stuck-up drama queens who pretended that their bodies were temples of desire. I am smarter than any of my low-paid teachers who could never make it if they had real jobs. I will rule the world. I will be known far and wide. I will live in a mansion and drive a Maseratii.

Mom will be proud and Dad will have to eat his words about my laziness and lack of masculinity. Those students who only like me for my access to weed, will beg me for my attention. They will come to me for my forgiveness and ask me for favors. I will look at them with an imperious sneer and wave them off with a flick of my wrist.

The bell rang for the first period class to begin. Live Pavlov's dog, I reacted. The old fears and uncertainties began to resonate through my mind and body. I'd ask Mr. Wilson for a hall pass to the restroom. I needed another fix. I needed it bad. It seemed like the time between fixes was decreasing almost daily. I hoped that I had enough with me to get through the day.

I heard Mr. Wilson call my name. "Mr. Hampton, will you please enlighten the class with your wisdom concerning last night's reading assignment? That's assuming, of course, that you've actually read the assignment. I do believe in miracles."

I tried to muster up some flippant remark. But, mustering was, lately, a lost cause. There was a time when I could muster with the best of them. I stared blankly at my tormenter. No words came.

"Mr. Hampton, are you there? Are you with us today? We miss you, Mr. Hampton. Where did your ability to favor us with a bon mot, facile repartee or glib retort go? We miss the old Mr. Hampton. Oh, Mr. Hampton, please return to us. We need a good laugh from time to time."

I hated this effete caricature of a man. He was the epitome of what a male teacher should not be. I slunk down in my seat. My brain could not produce a response to his humiliating remarks. I tried to dredge up something. I wanted to destroy him. My synapses were misfiring. I felt nauseous. I looked around the room at the smiling faces. They were mocking me. Even worse, some were feeling sorry for me. I was better than any of them. Not long ago, I had been the star of this class. I had the highest GPA of any of the 600 in my grade. Now, my GPA was sliding downward at an increasing rate.

I felt a need. I couldn't pinpoint what this need was. But, it was a need. I felt it in my bones, my tissues, every part of my being. It was an ache, a longing, an indefinable need for something. Anything.

I got up from my seat and bolted for the door. Mr. Wilson looked up from his textbook in surprise. "Mr. Hampton, where do you think that you're going? You sit back down immediately. You are a strange one, Mr. Hampton. I think that you should see the guidance counselor. You have a problem."

Yes, I thought, I do have a problem. I need a smoke. And, it isn't tobacco that I need. I opened the classroom door with Mr. Wilson's voice close behind me. I ignored the voice and everything else except my need to run. To hide. To be free from everything except the warm comfort of smoke sliding into my lungs. I fled out of the nearest exit. I had no plans as to where to go. I left the school grounds and ran down Ash Street towards the city park. There was a secluded area there where I often went to smoke.

I sat down on the marble marker that commemorated the founding of the city back in 1836. I lay back on the smooth coldness. I fished out the last of my pre-rolled smokes. I lit up. I mellowed out. I sighed with happiness. It was easy to be happy and free from worries. All I needed to do was to breathe in deeply and let the smoke do its thing. How could I have been happy before Toke-boy introduced me to weed? How could I be happy without his supply? My life depended upon it. I lived for those bursts of contentment.

When the effects began to wear off, I had only vague memories of leaving Mr. Wilson's class and coming here. He would be both angry and concerned. The principal would be notified. My Mom would be called. She would cry. I'd rather that she be angry. Even though they were separated, Mom would call Dad. He lived in another state. He wouldn't care. He never had. I hated to make Mom cry. I did that a lot lately. She knew that I had been acting strangely in recent weeks. But, she would never suspect the cause. In her eyes, I was a "Good boy."

As the drug wore off, a deep sense of melancholy set in. I had screwed up once again. The night would be filled with Mom's quiet sobbing. She would blame herself for my problems. I had tried to stop using weed. Each time, after only a few days without it, I called Toke-boy. He was always there for me.. He became my rock, my friend, my confidante, the father that I never really knew.

I got up and started off to nowhere. Darkness settled in over the park. I stumbled down the rutted path. One of the smaller paths led to the fish pond which served as the ice skating rink in the winter. The half moon was reflected on the water. I bent over and my face stared back at me. The face had hollow eyes. I winked, but the face didn't wink back at me. I stuck out my tongue, but no tongue showed on the water. It was as if I were that nobody that I had feared to be.

If only I had more smokes. Then, I'd be somebody again. I reached out and touched the blackening water. I splashed some on my face. It felt good. It felt like my mother's cool hand when it touched my feverish brow. She had comforted me through the ordeals of mumps, chicken pox and measles. If only I could let her comfort me again. But, to gain that reward, I'd need to admit that I was still her little boy. But, I was a gutless, pathetic teen age boy who was hooked on pot. I depended on it more than I depended on her. I hated Toke-boy and I hated what I'd become.

If only I could wash away that soul-less image which stared back at me from the dark waters. I leaned over further and splashed away at the mocking face. I felt the coolness engulf me. It entered my lungs like the finest of weed. Worries? I had none. Problems? They don't bother me. Momio, your little boy has come home all washed and pure.

FALLING WITH GRACE

Their faces were stained by a palette of colors. George Petty was a bright green. Peg, his wife, was a more subdued purple. Little Harry in the balcony glowed a bright red. Pastor Bob loved the way that the new windows livened up the sanctuary. Sitting on his padded pew just behind the lectern, he had a panoramic view of the entire congregation. Entire was, perhaps, the wrong word. Only a scattered few of the church's membership was actually in attendance. This was troubling to Pastor Bob.

Since his calling some ten years ago, he had seen the membership and the Sundays' attendance drop steadily. He wondered if it were his fault or was it a sign of a general decline in church attendance throughout the entire country. Irregardless of the reason, he took it personally. He had come here with the reputation of being a builder and innovator. His two other previous churches had grown and prospered under his leadership. Pastor Bob prided himself on being an agent of change. And, the change had always been for the good. Until now.

The organist finished the prelude and Pastor Bob rose to speak. He beamed his usual pontific smile out to the upturned faces. Most of them smiled back in return. Ralph Johnson was one who never responded to the pastor's attempts to engage. Ralph was an elder and a thorn in Pastor Bob's side. He could be counted on to vote against almost every suggestion that was made during the session's meetings. Ralph had even had the temerity to propose a new policy that would have prevented the pastor from charging for the wedding and funeral services of church members. He stated that "Those services should be part of the pastor's duties and he is being paid well for doing his duties." Even though Ralph was a relatively new church member, he had begun to influence some of the other members, also.

Ralph, he thought, must be being led by the Devil. Otherwise, how could he oppose him on every issue? Pastor Bob knew from his training that Satan had his minions in every church. It was a world-wide conspiracy to undermine Christianity itself. He would ask some of his most loyal followers to help him remove Ralph and his cohorts from positions of influence. God would want Ralph punished for daring to oppose an ordained minister on matters that only trained theologians understood. Pastor Bob considered himself to be only a humble servant, but he, also, knew that being ordained made him just a cut above the regular rank and file. He had sacrificed a lot to achieve this high position and he would not suffer fools who wanted to knock him down. God was on his side.

That night, he discussed this problem with Grace, his wife. Grace was a good woman. Almost too good. She brooked no deviations from the ten commandments. She was the bell-cow of the church's womens' association. She was the model by which other church women were judged. As a wife, she did her wifely duties in her sincere, by-the-book manner. Excitement and spontanaity were not in her vocabulary or in her actions. Pastor Bob knew that he had the perfect pastor's wife. But, he longed for a little panache and titillation. It just wasn't in her to provide those things. She even scheduled their times of intimacy. She insisted on Wednesdays at 10pm. If Bob couldn't keep that appointment, he'd need to wait until next week. So, the good pastor accepted his lot and gave the occasional glance to Iris, the organist's stunning wife. It was a good day when Iris glanced back with a knowing gleam in her bright blue eyes.

Grace agreed that Ralph and his followers would have to go. They should be banned from holding office in the church. If need be, they should be banned from the church. They had no right to disagree with the pastor. After all, the pastor was trained in all things churchly and his opinions should be paramount in the operation of the church. She would not stand for any church women to undermine her leadership of the women's organization. She might be small of stature, but she was big of conviction. She and Bob had been chosen by God to be leaders. And, by God, they would lead.

The biggest source of disagreement among church members was the matter of gay marriage. The denomination had taken a neutral stance. Each church could decide on its own whether or not to marry gay couples.

Pastor Bob had been vocal about his decision not to marry gay people. He was, after all, the one would be performing the ceremonies. The church elders had mixed feelings about the matter. Ralph was the most outspoken among those who favored marrying anyone who was a church member and wanted to be married in the church. At each meeting, the issue came up for discussion. Pastor Bob was tired of it. He had ruled on the matter and it should be a closed deal. He had received anonymous letters and phone calls about it. Apparently, Satan had reached the minds and hearts of those who wanted those sinners married in his church. He could not allow it. The very thought of him giving his blessing to those who were abominations in the eyes of the Lord gave him countless nights of sleeplessness. He had to quash this uprising. The end-time must be coming. It had been prophesized. It was up to him, as the church's leader, to bring this congregation back to God. And, by God, he would!

That night, he and Grace discussed their options. They devised a plan to discredit that apostate, Ralph. Ralph, himself, must be a queer. Otherwise, why would he champion gay rights. He had been heard, also, supporting Planned Parenthood and womens' rights to abortion. He was a dangerous man. God wanted Bob and Grace to remove him and his followers from their church. In the olden times, force had been used by God to destroy his enemies. Bob and Grace had been chosen to follow God's lead. But, how to destroy Ralph, was the problem. Ralph had been regular in attendance and had supported the church well with his monthly offerings. So, they couldn't use those reasons for removing him from their church's roles. They would need to find another way. God would show them the way. He always had. Hadn't they removed old Harry from the roles during their first years here? Old Harry had a drinking problem. He excused it by saying that he was lonely after his wife died and alcohol relieved his loneliness and anxieties. He came to church on Sundays reeking of the smell of the evil stuff. Ralph had the gall to recommend setting Harry up with a social agency to get him help with his drinking problem. Everyone knows that social agencies are just a liberal attempt to empower sinners and miscreants. He and Grace had persuaded the session to revoke old Harry's membership. It was good riddance when Harry died alone in a drunken stupor a few weeks later.

But, back to Ralph. His very presence weighed heavily on Pastor Bob. He sat in his usual pew each Sunday, his stoic demeanor being able to show disagreement and, even, disdain without verbalizing it. He was an irritant in his non-confrontational way. He didn't frown or roll his eyes to show his disapproval of the sermon or the supposed off-the-cuff remarks, but Pastor Bob could read the silent criticism. And, it annoyed him. Ralph was interfering with God's work which was manifested through Pastor Bob. God would want him gone.

So, in the dark hours of the night, he and Grace devised a plan. They would start rumors that Ralph was a closest homosexual. Grace would spread it among the women at their weekly workshop and Bob would whisper it to members of the weekly golf league. It might take several weeks of spreading and whispering, but it should have the desired effect. Ralph would be discredited and forced to leave the congregation. Then, Bob could look out on the stained-glass illuminated congregation with confidence and satisfaction. Ralph would not be there to taunt him with his accusing eyes. God would be pleased.

In the ensuing weeks, the plan was put into place. Those who heard the news about Ralph recieved it with mixed feeling. Comments such as: "Oh, I thought there was something funny about him." "Him, and his liberal ways." "You've got to be kidding." "I would never have thought that about him, I don't believe it!" "It must be a mistake" were heard around town.

Bob and Grace were pleased. He could tell that Ralph had heard the rumors and that he was worried. It wouldn't be long now until Ralph would be forced to leave the church and move from the community. God is just!

One morning, a few weeks later, Bob's secretary brought him the morning mail. As he sifted through it, he saw the return address of Jack Morgan. At first, he didn't recognize the name. Then, he realized that it was the young man whom he had befriended during his previous calling. Jack had lost his parents in a tragic automobile accident when Jack was only 15. He had been devastated and had been sent to live with his elderly grandparents. Jack's only other relative was an uncle named Ralph who lived out of state. The grandparents had asked Pastor Bob to provide some grief counseling. Bob had met with Jack many times over the next two years. He had always like to help young people.

They had become close. Perhaps, too close. Grace had been going through a lot of peri-menopausal problems. She had been too immersed in her own mixed feelings to give Bob any personal attention. Even the Wednesday "dates" were cancelled. She retreated into obsessive Bible study and self-hatred. He rationalized an excuse. It was Grace's fault.

The relationship with young Jack lasted until his grandparents became suspicious. They said if he left the church and the area, they wouldn't contact the authorities. Bob agreed readily. He announced to Grace that he needed a change of venue. He notified the church authorities that he wished to relocate. So, he came here. He came carrying a dark secret and a heavy load of guilt. He vowed to rid his small corner of the world of Satan and his minions. For, it was Satan who had caused all of his problems. And it was Satan and his followers who would be the target of his ministry. He came with guilt, but without the necessary remorse. He was not familiar with remorse.

He opened the letter cautiously as if it contained anthrax powder. In a way, it did. Jack had been having emotional problems since Pastor Bob left. He felt betrayed and disgusted. He, only now, had come to realize the enormity of what Pastor Bob had done. He admitted his own guilt, but knew that he had been vulnerable and in need of human contact. He had trusted Bob. Bob had taken adavantage of his youth and extreme vulnerability. Now, he wanted to go to college and needed money. In the letter, he wanted Bob to give him money for his tuition and expenses for the coming school year.

He excused his attempt at extortion by saying that God told him that it was only proper to do this. God punishes in mysterious ways. And, this was one way to punish Bob. Jack concluded the letter by a not so subtle comment that if the money were not forthcoming, he would broadcast the news of Pastor Bob's indiscretions.

Bob put down the letter, wiped the perspiration from his brow, and came up with a plan. He would withdraw a large sum from the bank and ask the church authorities for a new assignment.

In the weeks that followed, Bob waited for reassignment while the church authorities looked into some allegations about possible misconduct during his last assignment. He learned also that the money he had withdrawn hadn't been enough.

Ralph could still be seen sitting in his usual pew basking in the glow of the beautiful stained glass windows. Only now, instead of his usual blank expression, he sported a satisfied little smile.

SECRETARIAL DUTIES

"Take a letter, Miss Fulmer. And, this time, see if you can avoid spelling mistakes. It's embarrassing for me to have letters going out under my name with all of your stupid mistakes on them."

Mr. Corning said this to me without even the hint of a smile. He was serious. He was always serious. Oh, how I'd like to see the man smile just once. I could wiggle my ass for him and give him my best lap dance and he, still, wouldn't smile. There was no pleasing the man.

It's hard enough being a school secretary and dealing with those snotty kids and those pompous teachers without having to put up with this self-righteous, self-important principal. If I didn't need the money and the good retirement plan, I'd quit in a New York minute.

As he dictated in his slow, tortuous manner, my mind wandered to a dark place. I hated Mr. Corning. He belittled and berated me about everything. He called me dumb and scatter-brained. He made fun of not only my work, but my appearance. He called me the female version of the Pillsbury Doughboy. He said that my clothes were "Frumpy," like those worn by matrons twice my age. Once, in a worse than usual mood, he said that he wouldn't pat my butt if I were the last butt left on earth.

I should report him to the school board for harrassment and unprofessional behaviour. But, he was the fair-haired boy of the superintendent and school board. He had, to his credit, been able to turn a failing high school into the poster child of the school district. Even though he'd accomplished this through intimidation and bullying, they thought that he was worthy of a new five-year conract and a $5,000 annual salary increase.

Why would they believe me? I was a nobody. I'd been hired from an agency from among a group of less than stellar candidates. I was almost forty, somewhat overweight and less than stylish. But, I came across as being adequately skilled in typing, shorthand and taking dictation. The problem had become that when I had to sit close to Mr. Corning while he dictated, I grew nervous and that nervousness translated into errors while taking the dictation.

When I looked at his scowling face, I could think only of how I'd like to smash it, not of what I was transcribing. He had small piercing black eyes. He had a heavy black stubble that gave him the look of a hit man for the mob. He voice was raspy and contained no hint of warmth or compassion. He was all business. All hard edges.

"Ok, I'm finished. Now, check the spelling and punctuation. One more screwed up letter like the last one, and I'll recommend that the board fire your fat ass." He said that loudly and with emphasis. I hoped that the students in the outer office had not heard it. But, they were noisy as usual and absorbed in their teen-age angst and drama.

I left Mr. Corning's office still smoldering from his caustic remarks. Even the noisy outer office seemed like a safe haven. I sat down at my desk and looked over my shorthand. Much of it made no sense. I knew that I'd lost the gist of his remarks while I was thinking of how much I hated him. Well, he'll have ample reason to recommend firing my fat ass. If I didn't have my two kids to raise, I wouldn't care. But, jobs with benefits like these were not easy to find. And I, certainly wouldn't be getting a good recommendation Mr. Hateful.

If it weren't for Mr. Corning, I could put up with the other things. My fervent wish was for him to leave either voluntarily or be forced out. If I am to keep my sanity, self-respect and health, either he or I will have to go. I have no plans for leaving.

Slowly, a plan began to form in my mind. It would be risky, but the rewards would be life saving. I had no choice. I had to have the money and the security. My former husband, Eric, had left me and the kids with no money, no home and very little future. This job had afforded me my first glimpse of hope in many years. I had to keep it. But, I couldn't stay with Mr. Corning as my boss. He had to go.

I finished the letter as best I could. I took it into him and awaited the inevitable anger and insults. I didn't need to wait long. "Well, you've managed to produce a letter even worse than the last one. I didn't think that that was possible. How did you get this job? It, certainly, wasn't because of your looks. They are as bad as your secretarial skills. My God! You are worse than my wife. And, I didn't think that that was possible, either. I am surrounded by feminine incompetency. You damned women will be the death of me." How true that would be.

The plan became more clear as the week wore on. It seemed so right. So necessary. I began to smile more. I felt happier. Even Mr. Corning noticed my elevated mood. He seldom noticed anything other than errors or something that he could ridicule or put down. "Miss Fulmer," he said. "You look unusually fetching this morning. I may have to eat my words and pat your plump ass, after all. He gave me his version of a Grouch Marx leer as he said it. I thought to myself, Like hell you will. You lecherous buffoon.

To make my plan work, all the stars had to fall into their proper alignments. The wheels had to mesh together perfectly. The Gods had to agree to give me special dispensation. Some of what I planned would require their permission to act and their forgiveness after the act. It was frightening. Yet, it was strangely freeing. It made me excited and almost orgasmic. It was as if I had been held down, held back, stifled and muted for too long. It was my time.

His wife was his alter ego. They were a matched set. They were both finalists in the "Who Is The Meanest?" contest. She called him at his office several times each day. Her first words to me were always, "Get my husband, immediately!" I had begun to listen in on their conversations on my extension. It made me happy to listen to their palpable unhappiness. It would be fodder for my plan.

For the next several nights, I wrote and rewrote a letter to send to Mrs. Corning. I tried to emulate Mr. Corning's style of expression. Oh, I knew his style well. It showcased his mean spirit and lack of humanity. In the letter, I, as Mr. Corning, told Mrs. Corning that I had fallen in love with Miss Fulmer. I had been smitten by her shy femininity and loyalty. I loved her soft roundness after spending too many years with your sharp edges. I have accepted a new job in Idaho and she is going with me.

I timed the sending of the letter to coincide with Mr. Corning's week-long educational conference in Chicago. I would plan to call off ill during that week feigning a doctor's diagnosis of pneumonia. We would both be gone at the same time.

I mailed the letter on the Wednesday before the week of the conference. Mrs. Corning received it on Friday. Just after lunch on Friday she stormed into the school office unannounced. "Get out of my way you cheap floozie!" I moved aside readily while anticipating the approaching storm.

When I heard the loud bang, I had already begun calling the police.

PORPOISES AND PELICANS
- a seaside romance

I made friends in North Carolina. It was on Topsail Island to be exact. It lies off of the coast just north of Wilmington. It is connected by a draw bridge to the mainland. Back in the day, it was called Pig Island because the mainland farmers took their pigs there to graze. During World War II, missile sites were erected there as part of our coastal defense system. Today, the island is covered with expensive vacation homes. My wife and I spent many happy vacations there while sharing a beach front home with three other couples. But, those people aren't the friends of whom I speak.

I'm talking about the porpoises that swam up and down the coast just a hundred or so yards out from our beach. I'm talking about the daily flights of pelicans that flew over our heads as we sat on the deck or on the sand.

I don't know about the other humans, but those animals spoke to me. I kept this as my secret. My other friends already think of me as being a little strange. I looked forward eagerly to the arrival of my new friends that came from both sea and air. I heard the high-frequency chatter from the sea and bolder, closer quacks from above.

I could see that the porpoises paused slightly and turned their eyes to the shore. They looked right at me. I could see the gimlet eyes of the pelicans as they swiveled their heads to look directly at me. I felt at one with nature and at peace with all of God's creations. Seeing them and hearing them became a daily blessing. They were, I thought, messengers from a higher being. It seemed that we understood each other.. I wish I could have invited them for lunch. But, my housemates might have objected. I think my new friends understood. They never invited me to lunch either.

I made it a point to be on the deck or on the beach at what seemed to be our agreed upon times.. If I lingered to long in the, I could hear their louder, more annoyed calls from the air and water. They sounded agitated, even disappointed. So, my time on Topsail began to center on being available for them.. I began to listen more attentively.. I detected patterns in their chirping and quacking. I could sense when they were happy or sad. I began to talk out loud to them. My housemates overheard me a few times. I told them that I was just singing or mouthing the lyrics to some favorite songs. But, I sensed their concern.

Oh, how I longed to race through the ocean waves, jumping when the mood struck me or soar through air on the thermal drafts. But, I was stuck to the land with only my limited abilities to propel myself. We humans invent ways to mimic the speed and grace of our animal friends. We build surfboards, jet skis and hang-gliders to do what comes naturally to them. Those things work, but with much less grace.

Early one morning, I spotted my porpoise friends schooling just off our coast. The leader, I had named her Maximas, jumped high into the air. At the apex of her leap, she motioned with her flipper as if to invite me to join her school. I heard her now familiar greeting. I cupped my hands around my mouth and shouted, "Tomorrow morning at this same time." She seemed to nod in agreement.

Did I really make a date with a porpoise? I felt as nervous as any first-dater would. Should I take flowers or candy? Where would we go? Probably, a seafood restaurant. What do porpoises do for fun? I couldn't help but remember an old joke. "What did the Indian say to the pregnant mermaid?" He said, "How?" But, that joke might be as offensive to a porpoise as it would be to and Indian.

When the pelicans flew by later that day, I received another invitation. The leader of the vee formation, I had named her Polly, rotated her head, eyed me sternly and said, "Rumor has it that you are going on a date with Maximas. Is that true?" I bowed my head and plead guilty. Polly said that if I wanted to remain a friend I needed to take a flight with them tomorrow afternoon. I had no choice. I needed their friendship to balance my life between sea and air. I agreed to be on the deck at three o'clock tomorrow afternoon. Tomorrow would be a very busy day.

That night, I lay awake worrying about what to do and how to act. There was no manual available to tell me how to act on dates with marine mammals or birds. I worried about what to say to my wife and friends if I were gone too long. I usually took long walks both in the morning and in the afternoon. I hoped that I could stay within those usual time patterns. Of course, I might be invited to Maxima's or Polly's family. That might take a lot of time. Porpoises and pelicans can be very talkative. I'm sure they will ask me about my family background, religious affiliation and income. Apparently, they don't know that I'm married. But, in parts of the animal kingdom, that might not matter. I could have just refused the invitations, but I might never get an opportunity like this again. This could be a scientific breakthrough in the field of animal and human interaction. I might be the only human to have been asked on a date by a member of an other species. It made me wonder why I was chosen.

After few fitful hours of sleep, I awoke and took a shower. I wanted to look fresh and appealing. Bestiality was the last thing on my mind, however. Pelicans and porpoises pairings could be platonic, right? I just wanted to open new doors, find new frontiers. I might be written about in prestigious scientific journals. Maybe, a Nobel Prize was on the horizon.

I ate a hurried breakfast washed down with an energy drink. Just in case. I went out on the deck. No one else had gotten out of bed. I looked out onto the shining expanse of ocean that sparkled in the rising sun. I looked for the familiar dark shapes that each morning were backlit by the emerging sun as they cavorted along on their daily trips up and down the coast. I continued to watch and wait. The other seven occupants of the house were now stirring inside the house. Soon, they'd be outside on the deck and on the beach. At about nine o'clock, I concluded that I'd been stood up. Being stood up by a porpoise was worse than anything that I'd experienced in junior high school. I was devastated. I went into the house and into my bedroom. I shut the door before the tears began to flow. I composed myself and went out on the deck where my housemates were drinking their morning coffee. My wife noticed my demeanor and asked me If I were ill. "No," I answered, "It must be some bad seafood from last night."

That afternoon, when the others took their usual naps, I went out onto the deck and waited for the daily pelican parade. It was two o'clock and no pelicans. They always appeared at this time. Was I to be stood up by a pelican, too? This was a double whammy. Was nature conspiring against me? This was more than I could bear. I was devastated.

I walked out onto the beach and lay down in the warm sand. It was soothing and calming to be in touch with Mother Earth. With my eyes closed and my ears attuned to the sound of the incoming waves, I drifted off.

At four thirty, I awoke to find my wife shaking my shoulder and saying, "Wake up. You've been out here asleep for over two hours. You'll be burned to a crisp. What were you thinking?" What indeed! If she only knew.

She continued, "The rest of us were just talking about the unusually large number of porpoises who came by this morning and the bigger than usual squadron of pelicans that flew by a few hours ago. Both groups were making a terrible racket as they went by. We wondered what had agitated them. You missed both shows. You fell asleep on the deck this morning and you've been alseep on the beach this afternoon."

Had the invitations just been a dream? Or, did I really miss my chance?

In the remaining days of that vacation time, I never re- established connections with either the porpoises or the pelicans. They continued their daily commutes, but I heard or saw no signals. They acted as if they didn't know me. I tried to signal them to tell them how sorry I was to have missed our dates, but they kept their eyes averted. I could sense that they had been hurt.

There will be no Nobel Prize for me this year.

But, next year, I will continue to search the ocean and the sky for signs of another chance.

THE PYRAMID

Buffy spent all of her spare time practicing the school's cheers. The try-outs were next Wednesday. Making the football cheer squad meant the world to her. Really, more than the world. It was life and death. She *had* to make it. Her life would be ruined if she didn't. Mom would be devastated.

Mom had been the captain of her school's cheerleading squad. She had been coaching Buffy ever since she was old enough to walk. She had made Buffy a little outfit with a big "M" on it when she was two years old. The short little skirt had no trouble revealing her fat dimpled tush.

Mom made her practice the school's cheers an hour each evening after dinner. The jumps, wiggles and her childish attempts at doing the splits made her tired and her muscles sore. Mom hardly ever got angry or yelled at her about anything. But, she became livid when she couldn't seem to grasp the most fundamental of routines.

By the time that Buffy was ready to enter high school, she was already sick and tired of cheering. But, Mom insisted that she try out. The practice and drills became more intense. The anger matched that intensity. "Do it over! You will practice until you do it right. Don't give me that look. You are going to make Mother proud."

Buffy had stomach pains. She had headaches. She had trouble sleeping. Mom was relentless. The length of practices increased. The frequency increased. Mom had a weird gleam in her eyes as she shouted instructions to Buffy. Poor Dad realized that Buffy was a victim of his wife's desire to re-live her own youth. But, Dad never dared to contradict anything that his wife did or said. At night, when Buffy was ready for bed, Dad would talk softly to her and tell her that it would all soon be over. He knew that she lacked the skills to make the squad.

Sometimes, the girls who planned to try out would meet in the gym after school and practice. Buffy was reluctant to join them. She knew that they were much better. They moved through the routines with precision and grace. They jumped higher, were more rhythmic and did the splits effortlessly. Besides that, they were prettier and were much more confident. Even their voices were stronger and more commanding. She knew that she was doomed to failure.

When the day of the try-outs arrived, Buffy was scared. Mom found her crying in her bedroom. "Hurry up, Buffy. You don't want to be late on your big day. I've fixed a healthy breakfast for you. You will need all of your energy today."

Buffy looked at the big plate of scrambled eggs, bacon and toast. A large glass of orange juice sat at its side. She looked at the food and felt the nausea and cramps begin. She left the table quickly and ran to the bathroom. With her head over the toilet, she vomited what she'd eaten of her breakfast.

Mom called to her, "Buffy come down here and finish your breakfast. Do you hear me? I won't let you ruin this day for me." Buffy wiped off her face with a wash cloth and cold water. She went down.

She forced most of the food down while Mom watched disapprovingly. She was worried that Buffy would embarrass her in front of the other Moms who had been invited to watch the try-outs. Buffy wished that school policy would have kept the try-outs closed to observers. But, the Moms wielded clout with the school administrators.

Buffy got through the day's classes somehow. The try-outs were scheduled for four o'clock in the school's gym. She felt queasy and feverish. She thought of asking Shawn, her closest male friend, to take her for a long drive in that convertible that he drove to school every day. Maybe, she could entice him by hinting that she might allow him to touch her breasts. He had been trying to do that for a long time.

But, she lacked the courage to run away. She lacked the courage to do a lot of things. She didn't want to be a cheerleader. She just wanted to be a reasonably good student and continue her work in the school library. She didn't even like to go to football games, let alone be a cheerleader at them.

At 3:30, she walked slowly to the girls' locker room where the applicants were to change into their try-out clothes. Mom had selected a short little white skirt with matching silky panties and a heavy cotton long-sleeved dark blue sweater. Blue and white were the colors of the Madison Mariners.

Slowly, she got dressed. She looked in the full-length mirror. Her legs were too thin. Her breasts were too small. She had no butt. Her hair was too short. She had two large pimples, one on each cheek. Tears ran down her face. She rushed to the nearest toilet and vomited once again.

She had arrived in the locker room before any of the other girls. They began to arrive, laughing and joking among themselves. She knew only a few of them. None of those were close friends. Actually, she realized that she had no close friends.

One of the girls noticed that Buffy had been crying. She announced it loudly to the other girls. "We have a poor little baby here. Poor little thing. Wah, wah, wah!" All of the girls looked at her with amused expressions. A chorus of "Wah, wah, wah" filled the locker room.

Buffy slumped down on the locker room bench and broke out into loud sobs. Just then, the girls' physical education teacher came in. The laughter and the chorus stopped abruptly. The teacher said loudly, "What is going on here? The try-outs begin in ten minutes. Get dressed and get out on the gym floor. No more nonsense." She looked at Buffy, but said nothing.

Buffy thought of running out of the locker room and hiding somewhere, but she summoned up courage from some deep unknown reservoir and went out onto the floor. There was Mom sitting with the other Moms. Mom stood up and yelled, "You go girl! That's my Buffy!"

Before the individual try-outs, the group of hopefuls were to erect a pyramid. They had been told about this in advance and had been practicing for a few weeks after school in the gym. But, Buffy had not attended those practices. She hadn't told Mom about them, either. She had been afraid to be part of the pyramid. She was afraid of heights.

The other girls looked at her and decided that she would be on the bottom along with the heavier, less athletic girls. They told Buffy just to get on all fours and brace herself. Another girl would be getting on her back. "Don't screw this up or all of us will fall." A plan formed in Buffy's mind. She didn't realize it fully yet, but it was forming.

The woman in charge was the cheerleading coach from the local university. She blew her whistle to get attention. "The first thing on the agenda is the formation of the pyramid. You've been given information as to how we want it formed and the safety precautions for preventing accidents. You will be judged individually as to how well you do your parts. Pin the number cards on your sweaters so that we can identify you. As we say at the university, "Git er done, girls!"

Buffy walked slowly to the middle of the floor and knelt down on all fours as she'd been told. The other bottom girls took their positions. The second tier climbed on their backs. The third and fourth tiers followed. And, finally, the smallest, most athletic girl made her way slowly up the pyramid and posed triumphantly on one leg with both arms spread out wide. The audience gasped collectively at the beautifully formed pyramid.

Buffy smiled to herself as she collapsed flat out on the floor. She felt the bodies falling in chaotic fashion. She heard the high-pitched screams and the sounds of bones breaking. She looked over at Mom who was standing up with her mouth gaping open in a silent shriek.

Buffy felt vindicated for the years that she'd spent in appeasing Mom. Now, she was positive that she wouldn't make the squad. Tonight, she would sleep well after enjoying a good meal and a good book. She mouthed the cheer that she had made up for the occasion.

"Gimme me a B, gimme me a U, gimme me an FFY!" "Go, Buffy, Go!"

CALL ME LUKE

My given name was Raymond James, but everyone calls me Luke. I like that name. I've been told that I had trouble learning to talk. I do remember being sent to a lady, a speech path - something or other. She helped me to speak better. I guess that I still sound funny. Or, so I've been told. I've been told a lot of things.

When I started to school, kids teased me about the way I talked and, even, the way that I looked. When I look in the mirror now I see a thin scrawny fellow dressed in a flannel shirt and overhauls. That's how farmers dress. And, I am a farmer.

The teachers thought that I was dumb, even retarded, because I talked funny and was reluctant to recite in class. I cried when I was asked to read something aloud. But, I understand things. When I didn't, I went home and read about them in our encyclopedias. I cried a lot when I was by myself. I had few friends in school. I wasn't athletic and the jocks ignored me. I wasn't a good student and the nerds never included me in their weighty discussions. As for girls, they just looked at me and giggled and talked about me among themselves. I never had a real date in my entire life. Now, at almost sixty years of age, it's too late. Mom kept telling me that there is a woman somewhere out there just meant for me. But, if there is, she's kept hidden well.

I love animals. I went to the Ohio State Extension Branch nearby and earned a degree in animal husbandry. The local farmers used me to keep track of their cattle's geneology and milk production records. I had my own dairy herd and sold milk to the local co-op. As I've grown older, I have made a lot of friends based upon my unusual abilities. I've become somewhat of a local oddity for these abilities.

I have a prodigious memory. If you tell me your birth date, marriage date and anniversary date, I can meet you twenty years later and recite them all from memory. I know the dates and histories of almost every family in the entire county. I can recite from memory the breeding history of hundreds of area cows.

I've become skilled in photography and have had exhibits in many galleries and many fairs. I've gotten to know many Amish and Mennonite families and they have permitted me to photograph them. Which is very unusual for "Outsiders." I have become adept at woodworking. I make beautiful bowls and other items out of local wood. I have become an apiarist and take care of many hives. I sell the delicious honey.

I took up square dancing many years ago and have become very popular as a partner. I've taken part in local, state and national dance competitions. I did this to meet girls. But, the relationships have never gone beyond being a dance partner.

I think that I am popular. I sure know a lot of people and I think that they like me. But, I think that I am considered an oddity, not a close, personal friend. I've learned some magic along the way and I'm, often, invited to parties to entertain with my tricks. But, I go home alone. I really like the daughters of a farmer for whom I do some work, but they treat me like one of their brothers.

I fear that I'll go to my grave without knowing the love of a woman other than my mother who loved me a lot. I've never kissed a woman. I think about sex, but I've never come close. The square dancing makes me think of sex. Thinking is the operative word.

A few years ago, my farmer Dad died. He talked a lot like me, too fast and garbled. My sister lives quite a distance away, but we have been estranged for a long time. My parents didn't like her husband, so we never see each other. My Mom died just two years ago at age 90. She was a smart woman. In her life before the farm, she had been an executive secretary to the vice-president of a large corporation. In her early twenties she had gone to California to be the secretary to a major at March Air Force Base. But, she had resigned herself to be a good wife and mother and to forget her earlier dreams of a more adventurous life.

So, I've been living on the farm alone. I sold my dairy cattle. It was too much work. I've come down with some health problems. Lung cancer, to be exact. The doctors think it came from inhaling too much grain dust over the many years. I've had part of a lung removed, but, now, the cancer has returned and has spread to other organs. I guess that I'll be going soon to that great, lush pasture in the sky. I've never been religious, but this illness has caused me to think a lot about death and dying.

I am not sad, just kind of disappointed that I have never been married or had children. It wasn't even close. And, that is my biggest regret. My Mennonite friends take good care of me. I do have a lot casual friends. It's not exaggeration to say that I know almost everyone in the entire county. But, it's not the same as having your own family and some close, real friends.

How will I be remembered? Will it be as an oddity, a kind of idiot-savant? I think about things like that. When I looked in the mirror today, I saw an emaciated old man. But, inside, I think of myself as young, virile, handsome and the bon vivant that I aways wanted to be.

I've been placed in a Mennonite nursing home. The end must be near. I am not stupid. The kindly nurse and the aides tell me to not give up hope. But, I know better. Like an animal who senses death, I just want to be left alone and think my thoughts before all thinking ceases. I am getting many visitors, mostly local neighboring farmers and their families. The Mennonite church members from across the road come in often. My sister and her husband have both died recently. My uncle, his wife and his children are all that's left of my family. They've visited a few times.

I hope that the attention from the Mennonites has nothing to do with the fact that several of them have asked me about selling my 75 acre farm and its buildings. Recently, I signed a will that gives my farm, buildings and land, to the church. They've taken good care of me. It's good farm land and worth quite a bit of money for raising grain crops and grazing cattle. But, I've other things to worry about. Namely, my lost opportunities and my eternal soul. Not necessarily in that order.

I've been trapped by my peculiarities and my strange assortment of abilities. I've never fit in. I've been accepted, but not embraced. Oh, how I've longed to be what society considers to be "Normal." I've never held a woman in my arms. I've never rocked my children to sleep. I've never scored a touchdown or made the winning free throw shot. My life has been full of "Nevers."

I sought after love and acceptance, but found it hard to give love or even talk about it.

Considering my limitations, I guess that I've had a pretty good life. All that I've ever really wanted was to be part of that "Regular" group. I didn't choose to be known as the odd little guy who remembered everything. It can be a curse. There are so many things that I've wanted to forget.

It won't be long until I'll be buried in that little cemetery behind the Mennonite Church. I've told them to put on my tombstone only the word "Luke" followed by the words "All I ever wanted was to be just like you."

THE ROAD OFT TAKEN

I knew the twists, turns, hills and bumps almost by heart. The funeral processions had moved slowly over those sixty odd miles from the funeral home to the little country graveyard behind the historic church that was worthy of a Currier and Ives painting. My parents, all four grandparents and my aunts and uncles had all made this same trip. They all rest peacefully now in the sod of southeastern Ohio. It's a good place to rest. It's like a half-way house that offers respite on the journey to a better place. I had been a member of those trips. So, now, it was nothing new. I remembered the sorrow and sadness that were a big part of those journeys. I hoped that this trip would be more joyful.

As we made our way slowly through the rolling hills of this bucolic part of the state, my mind was flooded with memories, both good and bad. My mom awaited me. She had suffered for years, never able to enjoy a full and joyous life. I wish that I had believed earlier how serious her illness had been. My dad had died unexpectedly after falling from the roof of his home. We never had a chanced to reconcile or say goodbye. Grandma Jenny died mostly from old age and mal-nutrition. But she never lost her ability to cast out an aura of love. I found out later that she lived mostly on oatmeal during her latter years. Granddad Joe was ravaged by alcohol and tobacco abuse. But, he remained happy and loving. Grandma Margaret was dignified, stuffy and a little sour. She just died. Granddad Charles was even more stuffy and a lot sour. He just died, too. Uncle Lanny was my surrogate dad who taught me how to be a man in a world that values machismo. Aunt Mignon was loving and over-hyped on her daily consumption of twelve to fourteen cups of black coffee. Their two still-born babies lie beside them. They and many other relatives were waiting to meet me. I would need to apologize for being late to the family reunion.

As we turned into the little dirt lane that led to the church and grave yard, I heard the bell from the church's steeple tolling a mournful song. I had hoped for more up-beat music. Maybe, some salsa or reggae. But, I doubt if that kind of music is popular here. The procession stopped just outside of the church's double doors. Because I could no longer walk, I was carried into the church by some men whom I should have recognized. But, it was difficult to see from my angle and position. I tried to see who got out of the other cars, but I was already propelled to the front of the church near the alter. I guess that I'm getting the place of honor this time.

When the pews had filled with members of the procession and local townspeople, the preacher began his homily. It seemed like he was talking about me, but I didn't recognize some of the material. He must like to exaggerate. Most preachers do at times like these. I couldn't quite make out who, but a few other people rose and spoke briefly as if to amplify the preacher's words. An elderly lady got up to sing. She needed help to stand up. A young man propped her up while she sang "The Old Rugged Cross" and "Amazing Grace." It was rugged, but lacking in grace. Some of the people in the pews began to cry. I don't know if it was from sadness or from embarrassment about the poor lady's singing.

I tried to look around, but my view was obstructed by some silky fabric and a kind of canopy that had been raised over me. But, it was comfortable and cozy. For the first time, I realized that I was a little overdressed. I had worn my best blue suit, complete with white dress shirt and subdued tie. I don't remember getting dressed.

The talking and music seemed to be over. I sensed that a lot people were moving closer to me. They just looked at me, without offering to shake hands or give me a hug. Some said a few words to me, but most of them looked ill at ease and uncomfortable.

Three or four people leaned in and kissed me on the cheek. That made me emotional, but I couldn't kiss them back. Movement stopped and a blackness engulfed me. I couldn't see or hear. I felt that I was being moved. I heard the car's motor start up and we moved slowly over a very rough and rutty road. The motion stopped and I felt myself being taken from the car.

I heard the preacher say a few words in a boring monotone. I think that I heard some familiar voices accepting condolences from unfamiliar voices. It was all a kind of blur. Then, I seemed to be falling. I hit bottom like a runaway elevator. The next sounds were those of dirt and stones hitting the cover which had been placed over me.

Even though I was once a good writer, I don't know how to describe what happened next. It was beyond my ability to describe. I wish that I could be the first one to tell you about this experience. But, I am restricted, under orders not to divulge the secret of secrets. I can tell you this much. It wasn't what I expected.

FIBBER McGEE AND THE SLAUGHTERHOUSE

When my family helped to run the general store in Randolph, I had very few playmates. The little red-haired girl who lived across the road was the closest one. Going to her house required my crossing a busy state highway. I wasn't allowed to go across unless one of my parents went with me. So, by default, I played by myself most of the time.

We moved to Randolph when I was eight years old to help my mom's parents run the store. We lived in the small run-down addition to the store. We had no indoor plumbing. Our water came from a well that was ten yards outside of our kitchen door. Getting water required priming the pump and pulling its heavy arm up and down several times. Our toilet was in the barn some thirty yards from the house. An old-time two-hole outhouse had been placed inside the barn. During the winter months, we were in danger of getting frost bite on our bums from the long walk and the frigid temperature inside the unheated barn.

We used "slop-jars" at night to avoid the long walk. My job was to empty them each morning. I carried them with one hand while holding my nose with the other. My sister, who was twelve years older than me, escaped most of the household chores because she was commuting to the big city of Akron to attend business college. She was the first one in our entire family to go to college. Our parents and other relatives treated her like royalty for that reason.

During the school year, I was kept busy doing homework and stocking the shelves and sweeping the floor of the store. We sold groceries, meats, hardware, clothing, grain, fertilizer and assorted sundries. The second floor of our living quarters opened up into the second floor of the store. In the middle of that floor was a large opening which allowed me to watch the local farmers play chess and checkers while they ate crackers and cookies from large wooden barrels. Some them brought in homemade moonshine in quart canning jars to wash things down. One night, I brought my trusty pea shooter and a supply of dried peas to my observation place and shot a few old timers as they played their games. My dad came up behind me and gave me a good slap upside my head. I received several of those during my formative years.

My dad was known for his meat cutting and butchering abilities. He seemed to enjoy carving up beef and hog carcasses. He enjoyed making me watch as he wrung chickens' necks. One day he surprised me by saying that he was going to take me on a trip. I was excited. That seldom happened. We ended up in Canton at the slaughterhouse of the big meat packing company which supplied meat to our store. I walked in slowly, not knowing what to expect. The sounds and the stench were over-whelming. I wanted to go home, but dad told me not to be a sissy.

He took me over to where big burly men holding sledge hammers stood over a runway that cattle were prodded to walk down. As they came down the narrow lane mooing mournfully, the men hit them on their skulls with their hammers. Some cows dropped immediately. If they didn't drop, the men hit them again until they collapsed. I can still hear their plaintif cries and see their big brown accusing eyes looking up at us from where they lay.

The pigs had a similar fate, but in a different way. As the pigs scurried down their runway, squealing and snorting, the men stuck knives in their jugular arteries. They bled out quickly when they were strung up by their hind legs with heavy chains. Dad thought that I'd enjoy the spectacle. But, he was very wrong. I was traumatized. I still hear the thud of the sledge hammers as they hit the cows' skulls and I still see the squirting of blood as the knives punctured the arteries of the pigs. To this day, I eat very little meat. Even the smell of meat nauseates me.

I was busy during the school year, but summer vacation time was a different story. Aside from some mandated chores, I had little to do and no one to do it with. The little red-haired girl was too bossy and too much into dolls for my taste. Oh, once in a while, I crossed the highway to play with her, but she only wanted to play what she wanted to play. She did provide me with my first glimpse as to how boys and girls differ. When she bent down to play with her dolls, her little sun dress opened up enough for me to catch a glimpse of her budding breasts. It was one of those "Eureka!" moments.

But, mostly, I played by myself at my self-invented games. I divided myself into two opponents and tried equally hard for both sides. I listened to a lot of Cleveland Indian's baseball games on my Crosley radio and came up with my own version of baseball. I took the Louisville Slugger bat that Uncle Lannie had given me and gathered up a lot of stones from our long rocky driveway. I went to a position about thirty yards from the back of our barn. My target area on the barn had a Mail Pouch tobacco sign painted on it. I threw up a stone and hit it toward the barn with my bat. I marked places on the sign to designate singles, doubles, triples and homeruns. I batted for both the Indians and the Yankees. I tried to hit the stones equally, but, somehow, the Indians usually won.

When I missed a stone with my bat, it was a strike. When I missed the barn completley with a batted stone, it was an out. I kept statistics of all of the games. Each time that I batted, I assumed the name of a real player. At the end of my playing season, I chose a team winner and a Most Valuable Player.

The next game that I invented was played indoors along one wall of our small living room. The narrow area between the wall and the edge of the carpet was bare wood. The poorly constructed addition to the store had slanting floors which resulted in a sloping raceway for my game.

I took out my bag of marbles and arranged competition among them. I took two marbles at a time and rolled them up against the top of the slope so that they hit the wall at the same time. The marble that reached the bottom of the slope first was the winner. It was a single elimination tournament that produced one winner from among the bag of fifty marbles. I kept a written record of each marble's won and lost record and declared a grand champion at the conclusion of the winter season.

In bed each night, I listened to my radio until dad came in and pulled the plug. I listened to "I Love A Mystery," "The Easy Aces," "Fibber McGee and Molly," "Jack Armstrong, The All-American Boy," and "The Green Hornet." Hearing the junk fall out of Fibber's closet was always the highlight of my nights.

When dad silenced my radio, I got under my bed covers and read library books by the light of my flashlight. If dad came back to check, I turned off the light quickly and pretended that I'd fallen asleep tangled up in my bed clothes. That worked until he caught on and gave me one of his patented slaps upside my head.

One night, finding me under the covers, he accused me of doing something that, at the tender age of ten, I didn't understand fully. He said very loudly, "Stop playing with yourself! That's a terrible thing to do. You should be ashamed." Well, I played with myself daily and he didn't seem to mind. I was confused. It wasn't until quite a bit later, that I understood. So much for sex education in the 1930's.

My point is that, back in the day, kids didn't need much to keep them occupied and amused. We had no television, no computers, no video games and only a few movie theaters. Books, simple games, radios and talking to one another were our sources of fun.

I have kept my records from the marble tournaments and the barn-ball games. Marbles and stones are the permanent markers, the indistructable memories of my childhood days in Randolph. Those days ended for me in 1941 when dad got a job at Goodyear Aircraft in Akron. We moved to the Ellet area of Akron into a real house with running water and an inside bathroom.

Those memories, made from the smooth hardness of the marbles and the course hardness of the driveway stones, will remain with me as I go down the waning years of my life.

Sometimes, while lying in bed just before sleep overcomes me, I hear the loud sounds of those stones hitting the Mail Pouch sign on the barn and the thinner sounds of the marbles bouncing off of the living room wall. I hear, also, the creaking of Fibber McGee's closet door and the invevitable crash of falling objects. On bad nights, I hear the thud of sledge hammers hitting the skulls of sad-eyed cattle and the squealing of the pigs as knives opened up their arteries. Those sounds, both pleasant and gruesome, push me over the edge and into sleep.

COACH

"Drop and gimme ten!" Coach loved to shout this out to lazy or error-prone athletes. Well, they weren't really athletes yet. But, they would be as soon as he wore the baby fat off of them. He was a taskmaster. He was proud of his reputation. Kids were afraid of him. Parents complained about his rough treatment of their children and his salty language. He use his reputation to his full advantage. It carried over into his classroom where he taught his health classes in the same manner as he coached football. Intimidation was the main teaching tool for both of his jobs.

He was kept on as both coach and teacher because his teams had winning records. His classroom students all passed his health classes. He made it easy for them, but, mostly, he made it easy for him. His tests were based solely on the questions at the end of each chapter. His lectures consisted of reading from the textbook. He asked the best students most of his questions and let them expound on the material. He seldom prepared a lesson. He just said, "Open the book to where we left off yesterday. Susan, you bring us up to date. Eric, you read the first paragraph and Mary, you explain to the class what that means."

In that way, Coach avoided actually teaching. He considered himself to be a facilitator. He, even, had his two best students grade all of the test papers and record grades in his grade book. He had no discipline problems. This was especially true after he threatened to throw one young man out of the classroom window when he had the nerve to object to Coach's constant needling and teasing of Matthew, who had some obvious effeminate mannerisms.

Coach spent a lot of time diagramming new football plays. He read the strategies of the great college and professional coaches. He watched hours of films of classic games. He dreamt of winning championships and collecting trophies. He longed for recognition and acclaim. He had been a good high school and college player, but a very indifferent student. He was known as a hard-nosed, aggressive player who had a more than average mean streak. In college, he set the school record for penalties for unsportsman-like conduct. He took pride in that record. He felt that it was the mark of a man. It showed that he backed off from no one. He gloried in his toughness.

His language, both in and out of the classroom, was, often, profane and vulgar. But, no one called him on it. It was just Coach, being Coach. After all, hadn't his teams won the last three conference championships? Some faculty members and some parents objected, but most were afraid to speak up. The principal valued the trophies and championships more than he hated Coach's muscular posturings. The superintendent and school board weighed his demeanor against his winning record and deflected any and all complaints with a show of annoyance at the temerity of those who did complain. After all, Coach was an icon, a legend. He had put the school and, even, the town on the map. You don't mess with legends.

During the last game of the season, with the league championship on the line, Coach's mighty Bobcats played like pussycats. They lost 20-6 to their cross-town rivals, the Raptors. They not only lost, they stunk up the stadium. It was an embarrassment to the players, coaches and fans. They made mental and physical errors. They fumbled, dropped passes, missed tackles, forgot assignments and, worst of all, seemed to quit when they got behind in the score.

In the locker room after the game, Coach was livid. He yelled. He screamed. He cursed. He called his players, pansies, sissies, fairies and a disgrace to themselves, their school and the entire town.

When the team and coaching staff filed out of the locker room and headed for the team busses, they had to walk past the stands where many fans were still discussing the game. One angry fan, a former player, yelled, "Drop and gimme ten, Coach. You big phoney!" Coach looked up at the fan, smiled, and, to prove he still had it, dropped to the ground and began the push-ups. When he got to six, the heaviness in his chest made him gasp for air. He slumped to the ground and lay motionless.

The young men in line behind him and those in the stands just nodded their heads up and down and smiled.

DONNIE

Mr. Malone had a headache. He had a lot of headaches. He sat in his car for a while before entering the school. He had to ready himself for the day's onslaughts. Lately, most of his days had onslaughts. When he was younger, he met onslaughts head on and beat them into submission. But, not now. He felt the sting of repressed tears. His bones were tired and his blood ran slowly. He felt that he might not get through today, let alone the remainder of the school year. His thirty-five years in the field of education weighed heavily on him. He bowed under the weight. He longed to be free.

He looked at the sign directly in front of his windshield. In bold block letters, it read, "RESERVED FOR PRINCIPAL." He had always been proud to park here. But, no longer. His job had become drudgery. He had to listen to a multitude of whiners and complainers. He was tired of trying to appease them. He wanted to be free of them. He wanted no entanglements.

Reluctantly, Mr. Malone opened his car door and stepped out on to the blacktop. Students scurried by. Some said, "Good morning, Mr. Malone." He tried to ignore them. He hated the sounds of their adolescent voices. They grated on his ears. He knew that the students didn't like him. But, they wanted him to like them. They knew that his recommendations could help them win scholarships or get jobs.

Mr. Malone wanted desparately to be liked. He had no real friends among the students, teachers or parents. He shied away from bonding with anyone out of fear of being accused of favoritism. He wished that he had a confidante, a buddy or a pal. His wife had been all of those things, but she had died two years ago. His adult children would, occasionally, inquire about his well-being, but only out of a perceived obligation. He knew that they didn't really care. They only did what they felt that society expected them to do.

He entered the building, ignoring more superficial greetings. When he entered the administrative offices, his secretary looked up, nodded, and looked back down at her work. He went into his private office and sat down heavily at his desk. His wife's picture looked back at him with a worried look. This had been his sanctuary, his safe place. Now, it was his prison.

The day's tasks lay piled on his desk. Each paper seemed to look at him. He imagined that he heard them begging to be set free. Other papers and folders inside of his desk drawers and file cabinets clamored for the attention that they should have received yesterday, last week or last month. They seemed to say, "Read me, answer me, correct me or discard me." They sounded like cicadas ermerging from the lawns of spring.

He went into his private bathroom and looked into his private mirror. He saw an old face with a white scraggly beard. The eyes looked hollow and blank. Behind this image, stood a younger man, crew-cut, clean-shaven with a twinkle in his eyes. The young man seemed to smile at the old man. One eye winked. His lips moved. Mr. Malone thought that he heard the name, "Donnie."

"Donnie." Grandma Malone had called him that. His mother had called him that. But, in the past sixty years, no one else had called him by that name. "Donnie" had been full of life and hope. He didn't know then what he couldn't do. Prncipal Malone longed to return to the halcyon days of his youth.

The telephone rang, jolting Mr. Malone back to reality. The superintendent was calling. A parent had complained about her son's suspension from school. He wanted to meet with Mr. Malone and the parent today at three o'clock.

Just as he hung up the phone, his secretary came in and said that Miss Wilson, one of the new teachers, had sent a student to the office for excessive talking in her ninth grade English class. Well, Mr. Malone thought, if I were in her class, I'd be looking for even worse things to do to escape her boring lectures.

But, Mr. Malone played his role and scolded the boy in his best principal's voice and assigned him an after-school detention. It was what everyone expected him to do. It was his job. It was becoming more and more difficult to be someone that he wasn't. Now, if he could only figure out what he was.

He went back into his bathroom and stared, once again, into the mirror. "Donnie chose not to appear this time. Just a tired looking old man staring back at him. Maybe, he thought, if I try hard enough, I can bring him back.

The day went by like all other days. Just before three o'clock, he left for the superintendent's office. The mother was there already. She looked prepared for battle. The superintendent just looked disinterested. He had been in this scenario countless times before. Mr. Malone sat down, crossed his legs, looked at both of them with renewed confidence, beamed a boyish smile and announced loudly, "Heeeeres Donnie!"

GOING HOME

Jim sat there on the edge of the bed waiting expectantly. He wore his best Mr. Roger's cardigan, dress shirt, neatly tied tie and newly pressed trousers. His shoes were shined and his hair was combed and slicked down. His kind eyes and shy smile gave him the look like a proud father or a doting grandfather. He was, in fact, both of those.

If you were to visit this nursing facility everyday, on each of those days, Jim would be sitting on his bed, waiting patiently. Jim is a world-class waiter. But, what Jim is waiting for will never come.

You see, Jim is waiting for his wife to take him home. It is this hope, this dream, that motivates him to prepare himself daily for the event that will never happen.

The first time that I met Jim, he was sitting on the edge of that same bed in that soon-to-be recognized waiting mode. He told me that he would talk to me, but he would be leaving soon and our talk would need to be brief. "My wife is coming soon to take me home," he said with a smile and a twinkle in his eyes. "She's been in Louisiana and she didn't want me to stay home alone. I'm only here for a few days."

Since my first visit, those "few days" have turned into months. So, Jim gets ready and sits and waits, always ready, always dressed in his best "going home" clothes. It's not quite clear whether or not Jim's wife really did go to Louisiana. But, it is clear that she died several months ago. It's even more clear that he will not be going home.

Jim, despite his appearance, despite his ability to carry on a cogent conversation, despite his disarming smile and his playful personality, has a form of dementia.

Jim's reality has become distorted. His memory is selective. His today is a frothy mixture of yesterday, today and a dreamland kind of tomorrow.

He speaks of his childhood, his high school days, his college training, his teaching experiences, his military service, his long marriage and his six sons. The product is a bemused, often confused collage of anecdotes, some real, some imaginary.

How many other Jims, how many other Janes are waiting to go home? How many nursing home residents stay alive, stay reasonably alert and struggle to retain that spark of hope that they, too, will, someday, go home? How many force themselves to tie their ties, lace their shoes and comb their hair in spite of the aches and pains that those actions cause?

"Going home" is a powerful motivator for all of us. Whether its after a vacation, after a work-related trip, after military service or just after a hard day's work, we relish, we cherish, the thought of returning to our homes.

To many elderly folks, "going home" has religious connotations. Many look forward to leaving the travails of this earthly life and returning to their maker, whoever and whatever that means to them.

The doctors, nurses, aides and housekeepers who provide care for the elderly and the needy go home after each shift. Family members who visit go back to their homes. Let us hope that they understand the yearning and the heartaches behind that simple request, "I want to go home." Those words come from a deep place, a lifetime of memories, a lifetime of joy and sadness.

The person who hears that phrase uttered can help to ease the speakers' pain by listening and trying to make their sterile, institutional rooms a little more like home.

When I return to see Jim, he will be waiting still. He will be wearing his cardigan, his clean shirt and his pressed trousers. In his mind, each day is the first and last day of his life. It's the day that he'll be "going home."

God speed, Jim!

THE WELL-MEANING
SYCHOPHANT

Oliver was the perfect "yes man." He made a good living just agreeing with his bosses. He was, especially, valuable in the position of CFO. When the CEO or lesser bosses asked for money for anything, Oliver agreed readily.

He had nurtured this skill in various positions with several different companies. When news of his reputation reached the inner circles of major corporations, he kept receiving more and more enticing offers. He had been hired by his current employer only three months ago. It was the McQuacker Corporation, the largest manufacturer of crackers in the country. It was owned by the Ducker family.

The inner circle of management put him to the test early in his employment. The IT head asked for $10,000 to take a trip to Belize to check out their use of new anti-virus technology. Oliver agreed readily, even with knowing that Belize could offer little but white sandy beaches and crystal blue waters for snorkeling. The corporate team smiled in approval. Several other such requests were granted without question. The team agreed that they had found their man. The CEO even joked that if Oliver had been born a woman, she'd be pregnant every eleven months.

One Friday afternoon, the CEO, Donald Ducker, called Oliver in to his office. "Oliver," he said, "The management all agrees that you are doing a great job. We want to reward you with a little bonus for your hard work. We do have one special request, however. We do need your answer today."

Oliver recognized that a delicate situation lay ahead. He'd heard this kind of request before. But, being Oliver, he nodded his head in acknowledgement while giving his usual response: "I'd be glad to do anything that you ask, sir."

Mr. Ducker continued, "The company would like to place some of this year's profits in an offshore account in a bank in Bermuda. As you might know, the profits would not show up in this year's tax statement. We'd like to save that money for a year when our profits our low. We're fortunate that this year has been very profitable. I'm certain that you can handle this transaction with discretion so that the transfer of funds won't show up. When this has been handled, you will see a nice bonus in your next paycheck. Agreed?" Oliver couldn't say no. He was, after all, if nothing else, a loyal company man.

Six months later, the CEO and Oliver were sentenced to five years in a federal prison for fraud and tax evasion.

Somehow, Oliver's reputation had followed him. While in a detention center awaiting transfer to a white collar crime prison, he was approached by several heavily tatooed and pierced gang members. "Hey, cracker!," the leader said mockingly. "Wha's up?" Oliver looked down at his recently shined black loafers and choked back his fear.

The gang leader leaned in close to Olive and whispered, "We won't beat your white pasty ass if you give it up." Oliver had read enough stories and seen enough programs on television to know what he meant. His years of saying nothing but "yes" made his mouth form the silent assent. He could do no differently.

KENTUCKY

I hate school. That is the clearest thought that I have. Most of the time, my thoughts are incomplete fragments that make no sense to anyone, even to me. They bounce around in my head and get mixed up with each other. When I try to explain something, the words come out in random order. Sometimes, they make people laugh. But, mostly, they make people look away in embarrassment. They act like I just peed my pants. I realize all of this, but I can't get my mind to act like the minds of other students. I am a freak and I know it. That's the worst part.

My parents, even knowing my problems, insisted that I be put in regular classes even though a special class was available to me. I think that they call this "mainstreaming." I've never fit into any stream, let alone the main one. I hate it when kids smirk and laugh when I try to read aloud or attempt to answer the teachers' questions. My teachers seem to have been trained to treat all students in the same way. I get no concessions, no breaks, no mercy. I've heard about mercy in Sunday School. I could use some of that.

I'm not a dummy. I understand a lot of things. I read a lot. I listen well and remember what I've read and heard. I have ideas about the world, life in general and my life in particular. It's just that I sound and act like a comic book character. A badly drawn and written character.

I don't blame my parents or teachers. They do try to understand me and help me. I just can't connect. I must have a different polarization. My wiring must be different. My biggest fear is that I will never change, never improve. I fear that I will go from being a young laughing stock to being an old laughing stock. How can I finish high school? How can I go to college? How can I get a date with a girl, get married or have a family? Who would give me a job? My brain recoils at these questions. I am stuck with me. I am my only friend and my worst enemy. Sadness courses through my veins. I need a plan. I need a plan that only I can make and put into action. But, first, I need to get my brain organized enough to formulate a plan. That will require re-booting myself.

After a lot of thought, my plan of action will be to help my parents, teachers and peers to understand my problems. I'd like to help other people who suffer from the same problems that I do. It will need to be a very big plan. I worry that I'm not up to the task that I've laid out for me.

I lay awake last night trying to decide how to get my message to those whom I've identitfied. I couldn't just make a speech or, even, talk to them one on one. I'm not coherent enough. I need a bigger, more dramatic vehicle that wouldn't involve my speaking ability. When I got up this morning, I still had no plan. I had zero ideas.

When I arrived at school today, I went to my locker to put away my coat and pick up some materials for class. I noticed several large posters on the corridor walls. I walked closer and read the message on one of them. It said, "The Drama Club is offering a $100 prize for the best student-written play. The winning play will be presented as our feature production in May of this school year. Give your script to Mr. Blanchett, the Drama Club advisor."

One thing that I can do is write. That's how I get passing grades. My teachers are amazed that I write so well, yet speak so poorly. It's a giant disconnect for all of us.

I wondered if I could write a play that would convey my thoughts and still be entertaining enough to hold an audience's interest. Would the Drama Club even consider a play written by a well-known odd-ball? They didn't even let me work as a stage hand in previous productions. They told me that it would be too difficult for me.

When they see my script, would they laugh it off without reading it? Would the name, Frank Nelsen, be all that they would see? Maybe, I could submit my play under a nom de plume. I like foreign words like that. They sound classy. If my play, with my new "nom", should win the competition, would the Drama Club cancel the production if they learned who really wrote it?

But, first, my unreliable brain needs to write a play. I'll think up a catchy pen name later. Several sleepless night followed. Was I trying to do something that I was incapable of doing? Maybe, my computer could help me to line up some words in some kind of logical order. I didn't want anyone to see my work before I sent it off to the judges, so I worked silently in my room late at night.

By using a fake name, my expected rejection would not be made public. But, I would know and it would hurt me deeply. I wasn't accustomed to taking chances that might result in failure. I had failed many times before. I promised myself that I would give this play-writing thing my best effort. For one of the few times in my life, I felt a surge of confidence. I felt that I could do this thing. And, the feeling was good.

For all of my newly-found bravado, I worrried about writing something that would sound too preachy. Writing about handicaps and hang-ups were touchy subjects. It could hurt some vulnerable people. I would need to give the play some entertainment value. How do you make this subject entertaining? What had I gotten myself into? Maybe, I was in over my head. Maybe, I wasn't as smart as I thought I was. I'd never written anything for public consumption before. I had kept all my private thoughts just that, private. What if the play produced only laughter? Or, worse, sympathy?

The writing went slowly. It was agonizing. I had never realized how difficult it was to be a writer. Of course, I wasn't a writer yet. But, I did make progress. I tried to put into words how I felt when I was laughed at or ridiculed. I wanted people to feel my pain when I was teased or, even, bullied. I tried to use words that would inject images, sounds and feelings into their collective psyches.

I spent hours alone in my room, late into the night, thinking, typing and sweating. The work was made bearable by those few moments of elation when I looked at my work and saw that it was good. I stood in front of my bedroom mirror and tried to read aloud from what I'd written. I was surprised that those words seemed to flow from my mouth with unexpected ease.

At the end of March, a certain "Kentucky Wilhelm" submitted a manuscript to the drama club. Would the club reject it when they found no one named Kentucky on the school's enrollment roster? Had I out-foxed myself right out of the box? But, I knew that the script was good. I had read enough good plays to know.

The results were to be announced on April fifth. That would allow enough reherasal time for the planned performance at the end of May.

I waited expectantly. Through the school grapevine, I learned that Kentucky's play was being considered, but the selection panel was having trouble verifying that the playwright was, indeed, a student at this school. Should I come forward and reveal myself as the author?

The next morning, I strode into the office of the drama club advisor and announced that I was Kentucky Wilhelm. Mr. Blanchett eyed me with suspicion. He had been my English teacher two years ago. He knew me as a backward, shy boy who broke into tears when asked to read aloud or answer a question.

He looked me up and down and said, "This play is well-written and very insightful. As I recall, you, Mr., could barely speak. I doubt if you could write a play such as this one."

I wanted to tell him that I never had the chance to write one because he was too lazy to grade papers. He continued, "If this is your idea of a joke, it's far from funny. How did you know about this contest? Did one the club members put you up to this? If I found out who convinced you to submit a play, I'll kick him or her the hell out of the club. Obviously, you've copied this play from some anthology or collection of plays."

I told him that I had kept my original hand-written copy of the play and a copy of the typed copy that I had submitted. I said that I'd bring them in to show him if he didn't believe me. He face showed a gradual change from anger into a reluctant acceptance. "Okay," he said. "Bring them in and we'll talk. But, mind you, no tricks."

I hurried to my next class. I entered the room wearing a broad smile. When the teacher asked me if I could explain the significance of the Dred Scott decision, he and the students smiled at what they knew would be an entertaining disaster. To their surprise, I spoke calmly and clearly. And, what I said even made sense.

Their smiles turned to looks of amazement tinged with a little disappointment. They were losing their favorite whipping boy.

I was reborn that March. When people at school learned that I had won the $100 prize, they began to call me "Kentucky." It wasn't in a mocking way. Not only was I reborn, but I blossomed. It was good to be a playwright. I recommend it. Pick out a good nom de plume if you need one, and go to work.

WISDOM OF THE AGED

What one knows should be either spoken or put into action. I can do neither. It's frustrating to hear the aides and the occasional visitor prattle on about things that they don't really understand. I strain to make my mouth form just a few words to let them know that I could help them to comprehend many of life's complexities.

But, I sit mute and immovable in my wheelchair. People act as if I weren't really there. They never talk to me. They just talk about me. I've become like a pet. I get the occasional pat on the head and the offering of bite-sized morsels. I hear solicitous remarks and see heads nodding as they agree how good I look in spite of my infirmities.

I've been moved out into the hall along with a few other of life's throw aways. We look at each other in unspoken brotherhood. The boundaries of our lives are the wall of our cell-like rooms, the hallways and the dining room. Most of us need to be pushed in our wheelchairs. Our arms have lost their muscles. Walking is a lost art. My world has been shrunken down to the size of this floor. My world was once the world. I have seen and experienced much. And, that makes my present situation even worse. I accept that I can't return to my former life. But, not being able to talk about it and share it with others, is the ultimate blow. I don't want to be that old guy sitting in his chair who makes the occasional grunt to show that he is still alive.

Then, there is John. He's my roommate. It's not by choice. I had wanted a private room, but the place is crowded and I had the only single room when John was admitted. I don't like him. He smells bad and won't shower. He turns up the television too loud and doesn't even watch it. He likes to stare at me and stick out his tongue. I think that he is stealing my clothes. But, the administration won't do anything about it. He's sitting next to me now along this wall. If he sticks out his tongue again, I'm going to hit him. I don't care what happens to me. That's not really true, I care deeply. I still think that I have a lot to offer. But, I guess that I'm the only one who thinks that. I need to use the meditation techniques that I learned during my travels to the Far East. If only I could remember them, I'd close out John and the mean-spirited aide who comes in to check our room at night. I'd replace them and the other annoyances with thoughts of peace and tranquility. If only.

My big frustration is that my brain is crammed full of life experiences and the wisdom that those experiences gave to me. But, I can't seem to release them. I long to tell of what I've learned during my years of study and travel. I'm bursting with valuable stuff. Yes, I know that some of it is only minutiae. I've retained everything. I had always thought that, in my later years, I'd be able to regale a vast audience with all that I've learned in my ninety-plus years. I would command center stage and keep the vast audience spellbound and hanging on my every word. I would write best-selling books and donate the enormous royalties to charities of my choice. My family and friends would be very proud of me. I would be proud of me.

But, no, it was not meant to be. So, here I sit along the wall on the third floor of Memory House. What a joke! Memory House? It should be called Lack of Memory House. I sit with the other cast-outs. We can't talk to each other. We avoid making eye contact. We see ourselves when we look around. We don't like what we see. It's no wonder that our children don't want us to live with them. We aren't pretty and we aren't handsome. We smell of old age and death. Our teeth are rotting and our eyes are rheumy. There are urine stains on our trousers and skirts. Instead of speech, we make cackling noises. Even the aides who've known us for years can't understand us. Our thoughts, ideas and concerns go unrecognized.

So, I sit in a vacuum. Time is interrupted only by meals, toileting and sleep. Sleep is only intermittent. It comes in spurts of ever-decreasing lengths. My appetite is not for food. It's for human connections. The food that I do receive is a soft, viscous mash of things that old people can chew and swallow. I can still feed myself, but most of my fellow inmates need help. Even with help, they drool and slobber on their baby bibs. I look around the area and panic sets in. So, this is what it's come to.

I am no stranger to death. He sits on my shoulder waiting in anticipation. His beady eyes monitor my every movement. He is getting impatient. I feel and smell his hot stinking breath. I try to shake him off, but his claws hold on tightly. I am resigned to have him as my companion for my shrinking forever. My forever is no longer just a fleeting thought. Once, I thought that it would never come.

Time has telescoped into immediancy. Time used to have no end. It's difficult for me to accept that I have no real future. My future has been predetermined. It's a product of my genes, life-style, risk taking and luck. Once, I was able to look forward to new experiences, new understandings and new expectations.

Now, there is nothing new on my horizon and my horizon has become as close as the end of my arm. I live in the past. I drudge up all things old. I rework them in countless ways in my mind. I embellish them to add panache and a touch of adventure and excitement. Oh, the stories that I could tell!

If I talk too much about my past life, please understand that it is all that I have. I can't talk about that planned trip to Nepal or the sky-dive on my ninety-fifth birthday. I can't plan anything. Actually, I can't even talk about anything. I can barely get out a grunt. I feel over-stuffed with words and thoughts that are clamoring to get out. It's as if my lips are the iron bars of my own personal cell. They won't let my essence out.

Today, the warden of the institution planned a surprise for us. He invited a guest speaker of the "word." Oh, we've heard his ilk before. They drone on and on about getting our souls prepared to meet our maker and "getting right with God." Well, I think it's a little late. My past life will speak for itself. It is and was what it was and is. I can't undo anything. God knows, I've beaten myself up about a lot of things. I've asked for forgiveness not only for what I did, but, also, for what I didn't do. I don't plan to beg. I won't be making a last-gasp plea or a final confession.

In fact, I won't be attending this program. I will stay in my room and continue my reading of all of the so-called classics. They contain the reservoir of human knowledge and accomplishments from which I drink and take nourishment. I will not finish this task. But, each day I make progress. I feel the beauty of what man can accomplish and it sustains me.

I wheel myself slowly toward my room. I pass the eyes of those who no longer see. Oh, the eyes still work, but their connections to the brains have long been severed. The eyes track my movements. I no longer try to nod at the owners of those eyes. I never receive a nod in return. I've tried to reach out and touch their arms, but the arms drew back in alarm and suspicion. So, I pass as if in military review. Eyes forward, arms still, no emotion.

At the nurse's station, the eyes examine me for mental or physical signs of distress. Those eyes are both critical and solicitous. They are the eyes of the professional watchers. It's their job. I pass inspection and enter my safe haven. Luckily, John is still in the hallway. I feel gratitude for small victories. I take out "The Collected Writings of Ambrose Bierce" and settle down to read.

All morning, I have not spoken or been spoken to. I've only been eyed.

My room is nothing like my home. It's been scrubbed sterile. It is barren of warmth and coziness. But, if John is gone or asleep, it's quiet and free from the odor of death which emanates from so many of my fellow inmates. I give off my own odor, I'm certain. I've tried to avoid producing that "old man odor" that is so prevalent among the men who live here with me. But, two showers per week don't remove all of the odors of everyday living. I try to wash all reachable body parts each night before retiring. My arms aren't always up to the task. Some parts go unwashed. But, it's not as if I will be with a lady-friend later. I can't even remember that part of my former life.

Once in a while, I wheel slowly past Mrs. Wright's room and peek in to see if she is inside. She is old like me, but she looks pretty good. She keeps her hair done neatly and wears those flowerly housecoats. She smelled mighty good during the few times that we've sat together along the corridor wall. She even smiled at me. I smiled back. It's good to exchange smiles.

Oh, I have no illusions. She won't be inviting me to visit her in her room. She is a prim and proper lady. She goes to all of the talks by visiting preachers. But, she did smile at me. I have come to appreciate the value of a warm smile. Here, they are few and far between. I wish that the staff would smile more. I know that they are over-worked and under-paid, but smiles don't require much effort if you are young and healthy.

On some days, I feel as if my former life has determined how the end of my life will be. Now, that's a scary thought. I don't really believe in karma or pre-destination, but the birds do come home to roost. I wish that I could redo some things. If I did it over, I'd have been more loving and nurturing of family and friends. I was too involved with myself and my supposed important activities. I always had a feeling that I was missing things. I tried too hard to find those things. Ultimately, I found that much of what I thought that I'd missed was not really important. Soon after I found them, I realized the shallowness of my actions. I realized that what I'd left behind was what was the most important to me. But, damage had been done. Mea culpa!

In my current situation, what I miss most is R E S P E C T. I love Aretha Franklin's version of that song. But, who can respect a guy who, unknowingly, sits around all day with his fly open? It must look like an invitation. But, an invitation to what? I am no longer inviting. Once, I did have that elusive respect. In Tanzania, I was called "Baboo." In Swahili, it meant a wise old man. A baboon is the wise old man of the jungle. In Indonesia, I was given the title of "Guru." In Bahasa Indonesian, it meant teacher. I miss being give respect. I try to give it to myself. But, I know too much. I remember too much.

It's morbid, I know, but, I think often about selecting music for my funeral service. I've even made a CD of the songs that I'd like to have played. A few of them are: "Keep Me In Your Heart" sung by Warren Zevon, the "Intermezzo" from the opera Calvalleria Rusticana by Mascagni, "Ashokan Farewell" by anyone, "Hallelujah" by Leonard Cohen, "Do Lord Do Rememer Me" by Mississippi John Hurt, "Be Still My Soul" by anyone, "Meditation" from Thais by anyone, "Softly As A Morning Sunrise" by Los Indios Tabajaras and "What A Wonderful World" by Louis Armstrong. Oh, I forgot, "Somewhere Over The Rainbow" by Izzy on his guitar. That's a lot to ask, but I'd really appreciate the effort. I wish that I could be there to hear it.

So, here I am. It's the end game. It's the culmination of a life. How will I be remembered? Why do I care? Of course, I care. We all do. We all want to be loved both in life and in death. Does that mean that we all believe, in our various ways, in a life after death?

If I have one message to leave for you, it might be this: "Don't wait too long to give out love. It's like a gas that spreads out until it is exhausted completely. It affects the lives of all who are touched by it. It changes the lives of not only those whom you love, but those who have not been easy to love. It has healing power for both the giver and the receiver. It is, truly, the gift that keeps on giving."

I will try very hard during what is left of my time to practice what's in my message. It will be difficult to do that while sitting in my wheel chair being watched by unseeing eyes, longing for a little respect and a few smiles.

BABOO

I lay shivering in my sleeping bag on my army-style cot. I had placed the cot as close to the fireplace as I could without the risk of catching on fire. The African nights were colder than I had expected. Although we were near to the equator, the altitude of 5500 feet kept the temperatures cool in the daytime and freezingly cold at night. None of us had brought warm clothing. We expected a tropical climate. It was Africa, after all. Soon, we began to wear two or three layers of clothing. I slept in my blue jeans and sweatshirt.

We kept a wood fire burning day and night. In the daytime, we boiled water for drinking. Because of the altitude, it took longer to boil. Even with boiling, we had to add Clorox to the water to make it safe to drink. At night, we added more wood to ward off the frigid temperatures.

After a few days, African ennui set in. We became too lazy to do laundry. So, we began to wear our clothing inside out in order to show a clean side. My hair became limp and oily. We had no place or means to take a bath, so we just splashed water on ourselves occasionally. We all stank evenly, so no one noticed. The inside of my sleeping bag felt dirty and smelled of my dirty body. The worst part was that I didn't care.

Tanzania is a poor country. The world almanac listed it as being the second poorest in the world. We had no electricity and no potable water. We were housed in an old abandoned Lutheran mission home which was in the process of being torn down. Half of the building had no roof. Most of the inside walls had been removed. The rodents who had resided there for years, lost their homes and ran rampant throughout the building. During the day, most of them took naps. At night, they became lively and cavorted and played with abandon. The sounds of their toe nails tap-tapping on the hard cement floors kept us awake and watchful. Snakes slithered about, often entering our luggage and sleeping bags if we left them unclosed. I awoke one night and felt a movement along the side my thigh inside my sleeping bag. A bright green snake had sought the warmth of my body. Luckily, he wasn't one of the many poisonous kinds.

Our bathroom, the loo, was outside, some thirty yards distant. It was a pit dug into the ground and shielded on three sides with brush cut from the nearby forest. Because it was Africa, there was some danger of running into a variety of wild animals. It made the journey exciting. All of us tried very hard to wait until the morning sun made the trek less scary.

We had come as voluteers with the organization, Global Volunteers, to assist the inhabitants of this village called Pommern. Some of us taught in their school, some did manual labor on the decrepit classrooms and dormatories. The people in this high hill country were members of the HeHe tribe. They had fought valiantly against the Germans when they came to occupy their land. But, eventually, the area became known as German East Africa. Later, the country achieved independence and was re-named Tanzania.

My job was to teach English in the secondary school. It was a boarding school that serviced students of ages thirteen through twenty from a large geographic area. The students lived in ramshackle dormatories and grew and cooked their own food. The dorms and the classrooms had broken or missing windows and had wood stoves in the middle of the floors to provide heat. The regular teachers were men who had graduated from secondary schools and had completed a six-month course in teaching methods.

The students whom I taught had learned some basic English in lower grades. My job was to give them more advanced lessons in conversational English. The methods used by the local teachers were based upon the German model of education. Corporal punishment was used frequently. I, often, heard the sounds of wooden paddles striking bony, undernourished butts throughout the course of each school day. Sometimes, the punishment was to make the offenders jump in place for as long as five minutes without stopping to rest. If they did stop, they were struck on their legs with the paddles.

Students missed class frequently to help their families at home with the work that was necessary for their survival. It was a rare day when all of my students were in class at the same time.

Another part of my job was to supervise local workers as they attempted to replace glass in the many broken and missing windows. Our tools and the glass were of inferior quality. It made our work very difficult and very frustrating. The cutting tools were dull and the glass had built-in flaws. Most days were cold and rainy. Our finger became numb and unmanageable.

But, there were rewards. I became known as "Baboo." It was a title of respect. In the Swahili, the local language, it meant "Wise old man of the jungle." I liked the name. It felt right.

Our diet consisted mostly of rice, vegetables and coffee or tea. Only once in the weeks that I was there was there any meat. It was from a scrawny chicken which had been running wild throughout the village. The old lady who served as our cook caught it, plucked it and boiled it in a pot of water over her wood fire. She boiled it so long that it turned into a kind of mush, almost like chicken gravy. So, we had very little protein and no fruit. I began to lose weigh and muscle tone. The lack of sleep due to the nocturnal activities of the rodents and snakes sapped my energy and mental focus.

The sleep that I did have was filled with dreams. They were unlike the dreams that I had back home in Ohio. They were like Broadway extravaganzas. I awoke from my fitful sleep each morning exhausted from the excitement of the dreams.

My days were dull and uneventful in comparison to my wild nights. I began to live for my dreams. I moved through the days without thinking, almost on auto-pilot. I looked forward to night time to experience the next installment of the on-going drama. I began to make mistakes in judgment and have lapses of memory. I just wanted to hurry through my assigned work and get back to the more exciting events that took place in my dreams.

In my dreams, I was always Baboo. I was all-wise and all-powerful. I received adulation wherever I went, for whatever I did. I was the chosen one. My every utterance was considered to be profound. I was given the respect that I'd always wanted and never received in my real life. The local

Donald E. Smith, Ph.D

chiefs offered their daughters to me. Mothers named their babies after me. The best of local foods were prepared for me. I wanted for nothing.

When I awoke each morning, I lay a while in my sleeping bag just wishing for the night to come quickly. Even though the rats and snakes continued to plague me, the nights were preferable to the dullness of my mundane day time hours.

I asked everyone to call me Baboo instead of my real name. I no longer thought of myself as being anyone else. I had become, in mind, body and spirit, Baboo. I no longer needed to teach or do window repairs. I was the exalted one, the great and wise man, free from menial tasks. Let the riff-raff do that work. I was destined to lead, not to do the common work.

One day, a local elderly man, a kind of shaman, brought me a gift. It was the pelt of a baboon. It was soft and pliable. Immediately, I threw it over my shoulders. It was warm and comfortable. More importantly, I felt empowered. Now, I was truly "Baboo."

My dreams became more and more realistic. I loved to lie in my sleeping bag and await their coming. And, they came. They came in waves, waves that replaced my common sense and rationality. The dreams became my reality. I ignored my work as a teacher and window repair man. I walked around the village and out-lying areas wearing my baboon pelt. I could sense the veneration and admiration of all who saw me. What I didn't sense was their growing concern and alarm.

Some time later, I opened my eyes to see an elderly man with kindly eyes staring down at me. He sighed audibly and whispered something to a woman dressed in a white uniform. Dimly, I saw some of my fellow volunteers standing in a semi-circle behind the old man and the woman in white. I saw their looks of pity. I tried to get up, but fell back on the bed. The effort exhausted me. I wiped perspiration from my brow. The old man clucked in sympathy. "Just lie back down and rest. You have a fever. I think that you've contracted some kind of an infection. You need medical attention. My name is Dr. Werner. Your friends called my on the radio telephone. They are worried about you."

I tried to process all of this. But, my mind fought the process. I couldn't be ill, I was Baboo, wasn't I?

The days went by and, as I was told later, with no improvement. I lay on my cot by the fire soaking up its warmth. The baboon pelt was draped over my sleeping bag as I had requested.

Dr. Werner tried hard, but his many duties and the lack of medical supplies hindered his ability to diagnose my illness or treat my malaise. He served nine scattered villages in the Iringa region of the high hill country. He had no vehicle. He walked betweeen villages to serve his many patients accompanied by his wife who was a nurse. He apologized for his inability to make me well, a rare thing for a doctor to do.

On the seventh day of my illness, Dr. Werner leaned down close to me to talk in confidence. "I shouldn't be recommending this, but I have asked a local medical man, one of the village elders to come to see you. He is respected among the villagers for being able to cure many kinds of sicknesses. I suppose that he could be called a type of witch doctor, but I've seen the results of his work. What do you think?"

What I thought was, I love being a baboo, but it's time to go home. But, in this condition, I was too ill to make the arduous 8,000 mile trip. While I'd been lying there on my cot, I had felt the spirit and essence of baboo slowly leaving my body. But, I needed a complete cleansing. I couldn't go back home with even a vestige of baboo still influencing my thoughts and actions. If it took a witch doctor to purify me, bring him on.

The next morning, Dr. Werner appeared accompanied by a smiling Tanzanian dressed in a cloak of bright colored plumage. The doctor introduced him as Abd al Jabbar. I looked at the doctor with apprehension. "His name means servant of the comforter in Swahili," he explained. Somehow, I didn't feel very comforted. But, when in Tanzania ---------.

So, I lay back and told the feathered one to approach and do his thing. I had always looked for adventure and things that were out of the ordinary. So, there I was, lying on a cot covered with a baboon skin trying to recover from believing that I was the reincarnation of a once and mighty powerful baboon deity.

I looked into the witch doctor's eyes and saw sympathy and compassion even though his eyes lay in a coal-black face that had deep scars on both cheek bones. The face was attached to a coal-black body adorned with the plumage of exotic local birds. In spite of my initial apprehension, I felt comforted. Strange, how compassion and empathy can affect the one who receives them. Back home, in my work with medical students, I had tried to encourage them to let their compassion shine through in all of their encounters with patients.

I felt warm, strangely soft hands on my forehead. I heard unfamiliar Swahili words being said in a lilting, melodic voice. I felt warmth emanating from his hands. My body relaxed and my head felt a release from the pressure and constriction that I had felt for many days. It might sound odd, but the total experience brought me a sense of peace and freedom. It was as if I had an out-of-body happening, a catharsis of sorts. I felt calm and happy. The baboon's clamoring stopped and the false energizing that he had produced in me receded into only a dim memory.

Later, I was told that the on-lookers had witnessed a dramatic change in my look and behavior. I changed from a manic psuedo-baboon back into my normal self. They were glad to have me back. I was glad to be back, too.

But, on some days, I remember my days as "Baboo," the once and mighty wise old man of the high hill country of Tanzania. Those memories bring a smile and a sense of relief. I had come close to allowing him to take over.

RELATIVES AND
OTHER ODDITIES

Steve spent most of his time being embarrassed. He didn't cause the embarrassment, his relatives did. He compared them to the characters in one of his favorite books, "A Confederacy Of Dunces."

When he was growing up, his parents were to blame. He dad was a mousey little man who always word a dark suit, white dress shirt and a black tie. Often, he wore an old-fashioned fedora. His hair was slicked back with something that smelled like the lard Steve's granddad made from pork belly. He was a laborer in the local pottery, but he liked to dress up and pretend that he was someone important like a banker or lawyer. But, he wasn't.

Mom, on the other hand, liked to dress like a teeny-bopper. She wore mini-skirts that revealed too much of her white fleshy thighs that were laced with dark blue varicose veins. She had medically induced puffy lips that were painted in the brightest of reds. Her long false eyelashes floated demonically above her black eye liner.

When his mom and dad went out together, which was seldom, they looked like they didn't belong with each other. In fact, they didn't. Mom went her way and dad went his. Mom's way was nights out with the girls, usually, to a bar that had dancing. The local male bar patrons knew her well. She was thought to be an easy mark. Steve didn't know this for certain, but he's heard the rumors.

Dad's idea of going out was a trip to the library or to the local Odd-Fellows Hall where he was a founding member. So, the two of them seldom were seen together. It was just as well because when they were together, they argued over everything.

Steve seldom went anywhere with them. He hated the way that they looked and the way that they acted. When he was in school, the kids who knew his parents teased and taunted him. "Your dad is a pansy and your mom is a whore." And, those were the kindest of the many comments.

So, Steve grew up trying desparately to ignore and, even, avoid his parents. It didn't make for a happy home life. He envied those kids whose parents made happy homes for their children, just like those on the heart-warming television shows. He spent a lot of time at the home of his best friend, Howard. Howard's dad was a fireman whose hearty laugh could fill a room. He always slapped Steve on the back and asked loudly, "How ya doin Stevie?" Howard's mom always had milk and cookies ready when Steve came to visit. She looked like a real mother. Her crisply starched aprons covered bright flowery dresses. She always asked Steve how he was feeling and inquired about the health of his parents. He lied and told her that they were fine. In reality, it had been a long time since they were fine, if they ever had been.

Steve' sister, Lois, seemed to have come from a different family. At an early age, she had began dating older men. Oh, wait! She did resemble her mother. But, unlike her mother, she was multi-talented and was driven to become rich and famous. She was a good artist, gourmet cook, talented pianist and had an adventurous streak. She had been to Chicago, New York City and Baltimore with her great aunt. That auntie was the real character of the family. More about her later. Lois earned a degree in business and moved to California to work when she was twenty-one. After World War II, she returned to Ohio and, to the surprise of all who knew her, married a farmer, had two children, forgot her earlier dreams and never looked back. Was that a happy ending to her story or a kind of tragedy? When she died at age 92, she seemed happy.

Steve's two sets of grandparents were completely and totally different. His dad's parents were poor all of their married life. Granddad never held a regular job. He was a kindly, gentle alcoholic who chewed Mail Pouch tobacco and spit his tobacco juice int an ever-present spitoon. He had the occasional odd-job as a handyman who wasn't very handy. Grandma was your stereotypical grandma. She wore her white hair in a severe bun on top of her head. She had been a school teacher before marrying Grandpa Joe. She supported granddad and their two children by taking in sewing jobs. Steve loved them because they loved him. And, they oved each other. Sometimes, he stayed overnight with them and slept between them in their only bed. Steve's parents were appalled at this. Finally, they forbade him to stay overnight. Soon after that, their ramshackle little house on First Street collapsed on itself. Over the compaints of Steve's mom, dad bought his parents a little house near the feed mill and railroad tracks. They died in their mid-eighties from old age and the neglect of basic health needs. Steve felt genuine grief for the first time.

His maternal grandparents were a different story. Somehow, in spite of their dour, ascerbic personalities, they had acquired quite a bit of wealth. They owned a general store, three apartment buildings and two single-family homes. Steve didn't really know them. They were difficult to know. They didn't encourage closeness or intimacy of any kind. Somehow, in spite of this, they managed to have two children. Steve's mom's brother, Charles, died at age thirty-two during a routine appendectomy. He had married a Catholic woman who was five years his senior. His parents were aghast and promptly stopped all contact with him, his wife and their daughter Peggy Lou.

As you might guess, the grandparents were very openly prejudiced when it came to Negroes, Jews, Catholics and people of any ethnic group other than caucasian. Charles is buried beside his wife in a Catholic cemetery. Steve's grandparents didn't attend Charles' funeral and never visited his grave. When Peggy Lou tried to contact her grandparents, she was rebuffed by them and was told not to bother them any more.

When Steve told me about Charles and Peggy Lou, he broke down and cried. Even sadder was the fact that this story, these attitudes, were not uncommon back in those days.

Steve only visited his mom's parents a few times before they died. They lived in a large three-story Victorian style home. Each of the ten rooms had its own fireplace. They only lived on the bottom floor, but the entire house was filled with expensive antiques. He had never received a hug, a kiss or a compliment from either of them. In contrast to the terrible sadness which he'd felt when his other grandparents died, he felt nothing when they died. The only good thing that he could attribute to them was that his mom inherited a nice house in the big city of Akron.

Steve's family was not large, so there's not a whole lot else to tell you about his relatives, but, he did tell a few more stories about some other interesting characters.

His dad's sister, Mignon, was married to a good old boy from the mountains of West Virginia. His name was Lannie. Lannie had brothers named French, Stanton and Conrad. Mignon was a good-natured woman who opened her house and her heart to Steve during his frequent overnight stays with them. Their two children died at child-birth. Steve became a kind of surrogate son. Aunt Mignon loved to tell the story of the time he slipped down into the basement and starched her underwear while they were still in the washing machine. Mignon was a coffee fanatic. She, usually, drank twelve to fourteen cups each day. But, Steve said, she never appeared to over-caffeinated. Lannie and Mignon both loved children. Steve said that he was the lucky recipient of their love.

Uncle Lannie became Steve's role model for being a man, husband and provider. He worked hard in the steel mills of Canton and painted houses as a second job. He took loving care of Mignon and adored children and animals. He took Steve on many hunting and fishing trips. He taught him how to shoot and how to catch fish in the most unlikely of places. Steve told me how Lannie insisted on fishing only with live bait. So, very early on the mornings of their fishing trips, they would stop and seine for minnows in the creeks along the way and cut down roadside weeds to look for the fat, juicy bugs that lived in the stalks. They always caught fish.

Hunting with intent to kill, was not something that Steve really liked. Lannie had grown up in West Virginia needing to kill to put food on their table. Under Lannie's tutilege, Steve learned to handle guns and shoot them with accuracy. But, when he shot his first rabbits, squirrels and groundhogs, he was saddened by the sight of the still squirming animals. He was moved to tears by their plaintiff cries.

What really traumatized Steve was when he shot and wounded a doe on a trip to Pennsylvania. The deer was not dead when Steve found her lying in the bushes. She looked up at Steve with her big brown eyes. Her mouth seemed to form the question, "why?"

Lannie told Steve that the kindest thing to do would be to shoot her in the head to end her suffering. He asked Steve, as the shooter, to do it. Steve said that he turned away crying and ran into the woods. Lannie shot the deer, found Steve and told him that it was okay to feel that way. Some people, he said, were not meant to be hunters. He never teased or embarrassed Steve by telling this story.

Lannie made gloves, a cap and a vest out of the deer's hide. Steve kept a pair of gloves for years to remind him of the day that he decided not to be a hunter of any living creature unless that creature threatened his life or the lives of other human beings.

The real character in Steve's family was his sister's son, James. He was born early and spoke and walked much later than normal. He had a speech defect and was taken to a speech pathologist at an early age. He seemed to lack social skills and, at first, was thought to have some form of retardation. But, soon, his parents and teachers realized that he absorbed and retained enormous amounts of information. His brain stored all of the sensory information that was given to it.

But, he had to endure the teasing of insensitive people because of his awkward appearance and speech patterns. He graduated from high school and a branch of The Ohio State University with a major in animal husbandry. He became known throughout Ohio's Amish and Mennonite community as a keeper of cattle milking and breeding records. He kept most of this information in his head. He was equally famous for remembering people's birthdays, anniversaries and wedding dates. If he met you ten years ago and hadn't seen you since, he could remember your name and all of the important dates in your life.

Later in life, he took ujp woodworking, photography, bee-keeping and magic. He became skilled in all of these areas. He made beautiful prize-winning wooden bowls. His photographs of Amish life won many awards at fairs and photo competitions. He won the confidence of Amish families who, usually refused to be photographed. His honey won awards at the county fairs. He joined a square-dancing club that won awards in national contests. He became skilled in all that he attempted. In addition to all of those hobbies, he ran a dairy farm and sold milk to local co-ops.

He never had a real girl friend, never married, never had children. People respected him, admired him, loved him, but, in spite of his many talents, they still thought of him as being odd. He died at age sixty from complications of lung cancer. Hundreds attended his funeral in the local Mennonite church. It was an unusual honor for one who was not a Mennonite. Steve was among the many who watched his body being lowered into the simple grave in the windswept field behind the church. Bonneted and shawl-draped women placed flowers on his casket as it dropped slowly into the fertile soil. Steve said that he heard the keening of the women and felt the increased velocity of the wind as the up-turned sod reclaimed one its own.

Steve took a few minutes to regain his composure. He had been very fond his nephew. He brightened up as he told me of his great-aunt Mae, his family's society maven. She was his sour grandma's younger sister. She met and married a wealthy Chicago dentist. They lived in Chicago, New York City and Baltimore among a few lesser places. After "Doc Kerr" died, she traveled the country in style on the ample funds that he'd left her. They had one son, Kenneth, who, in his own right, was wealthy, also. So, she didn't have any money worries. She shopped in the most exclusive stores, attended opera and ballet performances in the best venues and ate at most of the country's five-star restaurants. Once in a while, she stopped to see her sister and her husband, my sour grandparents. Usually, she brought everyone gifts. Expensive gifts. She distributed them in her haughty, condescending manner. It was obvious to Steve that she felt pity, not love, for her poor, unfortunate relatives.

Steve admitted that she seemed to favor him over the rest of the family. She seemed to like boys and men over girls and women. She had that reputation. Steve's parents didn't want Steve to visit with her alone. Steve had developed some teen age acne on his face. Aunt Mae said that she had an expensive astringent which would clear up his blemishes. She was staying temporarily in some rented rooms close to Steve's home. She told him to stop in after school to get some of the liquid. Without telling his parents, he stopped to find her lying in bed wearing a nightgown. It was one of those low cut flimsy things that showed a lot of cleavage. She motioned for Steve to come over to her so that she could wipe some of the astringent on his cheeks.

Reluctantly, Steve went over and sat down on the edge of the bed. She patted him on the cheeks and began the treatment. When she finished, she said that he looked tired and that he could lie down and rest a while beside her. Steve felt conflicted. She was not unattractive in a hard kind of way, but she was his aunt. He felt his face flush and it wasn't because of the astringent. He got up, made a quick excuse that he was expected at home, and left the room hurriedly. As he walked home, he realized that the rumors might, in fact, be true.

At age 92, Aunt Mae mistook a cemetery driveway for her brother's driveway and knocked over three tombstones. After paying the township for the cost of replacing the stones, she decided, reluctantly, to give up driving. She died at age 94 in a nursing home where she had been accused of flashing some of the older male residents, two of whom died of cardiac arrests.

Steve told me more stories of his motley crew of relatives, but I'd heard enough. They reminded me of my own family. The memories were too painful for me to hear more.

MOONLIGHT AND
HOBBY HORSES

I'd been inside the jungle almost two weeks when the jungle got inside of me. I was teaching English in the little jungle village of Jeruk Legi. The name meant "Sweet Orange" in the Bahasa Indonesian language. Well, they did grow a lot oranges, but the place was certainly not sweet. Six other Americans and I had been living in a decrepit dormitory once used to house the local teaching staff. The local teachers had refused to live there any longer so a new dormitory was built for them. The school officials must have felt that the old one was suitable for us American educators. It had no electricity, no running water, no flush toilets and no business housing anyone.

Snakes, rats and lizards ran amok. The heat and humidity were stifling. They sapped all of our creative thought and energy. I longed for the uncertainties of Ohio weather. I longed to go home. The school building was not much better. Most of the windows had been broken. The chalkboards had missing sections. The desks had missing or broken legs and wobbled back and forth. The textbooks for my English classes were tattered, outdated and had scribbled remarks on every page. The books had been donated by American publishers from stockpiles of books which had been returned by American teachers. Pages were missing and typos abounded.

The students from the village and those who were bussed in from the outlying areas arrived each morning sleepy-eyed and unprepared for the day's lessons. The few who seemed interested inspired me to overcome the tropical malaise. I had to feign enthusiasm. The nights were long and sweaty. I awoke each morning drenched in my own fluids. Geckoes scurried around on the walls and ceiling looking for the swarms of insects. They provided a much needed distraction from the oppressive heat and humidity. I lay awake often watching them catch and devour the clouds of flying bugs. But, new clouds kept rolling in.

Guntar, one of the local Indonesian teachers, approached me after school and asked me if I wanted to attend a special ceremony that night. He explained that each month when the moon was full, the village would gather at a site in the deepest part of the jungle. The village elders had asked him to invite our group of volunteers. He said that it was an honor not usually bestowed upon outsiders. He assured me that it would be an enlightening experience. I said that I would relay his invitation to my colleagues. We had all agreed that we would try to absorb as much of the village culture as we possible could in our limited time with them.

After our supper that night, our group met with the local teachers and most of the villagers at the trail head that led to the site of the ceremony. I asked Guntar to tell me more about what to expect, but he said that it was difficult to explain. We'd need to experience it first hand. He had a strange look on his face as he said this.

It was growing dark and the dense foliage prevented the last rays of sunlight from lighting our way through the jungle. We had to hold on to the ones in front of us to walk without stumbling over the rocks and tree roots. Our clothing was snagged by the tree branches which extended out over the path. We began to mumble among our selves as to why we had agreed to take part in this journey.

Through an opening high above the palms, I saw the full moon. It seemed larger than the full moons back home in Ohio. Instead of the usual happy face, this moon seemed to have a sinister scowl. When the villagers saw the moon, I could hear their murmors of anticipation. Or, was it trepidation? I whispered to Keith, one of my fellow American teachers, "What have we gotten ourselves into?" He responded with a barely audible, "I don't know, but it's a little too spooky for me."

The path wove in and out and around and about. Once in a while, the moon appeared in the openings of the canopy. In spite of its scowl, it seemed to be beckoning us onward. Becky, one of our women teachers, said loudly, "I'm going back! This is beginning to frighten me." One of the village elders shouted back very gruffly, "There is no turning back now.

The Gods will not permit it." Now, I was spooked. I did not like being forced down a path at the insistance of their alien Gods. I found Guntar among the pack and told him that we Americans wanted to go back to the miserable, but safe confines of our dormitory. In tones that I'd not heard from him before, Guntar said loudly, "We cannot permit you to leave. The Gods are expecting you. We've given them your names in advance. Now, stay in line and keep moving!"

We Americans looked at each other in shocked surprise. I saw fear in their eyes. I sensed the fear in mine. Finally, we came to an opening in the form of a large grassy circle. It was illuminated by the huge orb which was now directly over us.

On one side of the circle, sat a row of village elders. Looking closer, I saw that they all wore masks. We had seen these masks in the elders' meeting room back in the village.

On the other side of the area, a gamelan orchestra sat on the ground in front of their instruments. In the center, stood a large table covered with an assortment of herbs and hollowed out coconut shells. The shells contained a brownish liquid. Leaning against the table, was a row of what looked like the old-fashioned hobby horses. I remembered riding one when I was very young. I wished that I were young once again.

We Americans like our God to be in human form. We like His recognizable face to smile down on us with benevolence. We don't like our God to be frightening. We like to be comforted. If this was religion, I decided, at that moment, to stick with Christianitiy.

We were told to sit on the ground near the elders. I was long past the age when sitting cross-legged on the ground was comfortable.. The chief elder rose and made an announcement in Bahasa. I understood only part of it. But, I gathered that the lunar ritual would begin soon. He raised his arms in salute to the enormous moon. As he took his seat, the gamelan orchestra began to play. The sound reminded me of our xylaphones. It was soothing and melodic. Soothing was what our group of Amerians needed badly. In spite of ourselves, we began to sway to the hypnotic sound along with the villagers.

The chief elder made another announcement. The Indonesians lined up and walked slowly to the table. Each one took a few leaves from the herbs and a liquid-filled coconut shell. After they had done this, they returned to their seats and began to chew the leaves and drink the liquid. We Americans remained seated and watched in fascination.

Soon, the ambiance changed from tranquility to electricity. Masks were passed out when the assembly had finished eating and drinking. The masked ones arose from their seats and began to gyrate frantically in time to the music. When the gyrations reached a manic level, they mounted hobby horses and galloped around the circle neighing and snorting loudly. Some of the riders fell over in a stupor, eyes glazed, staring up at the moon in supplication and wonderment. The moon looked down with approval.

Guntar came over and told us that it was our turn. It was obvious that the leaves and the liquid were opiates. The dancers were highly intoxicated. Many were hallucinating. We Americans hesitated. How dangerous were those substances? Should we go along with the crowd? Did we have a choice? Guntar said sternly, "You have lived in this village, in this country, because we permitted it. You have received our food and our lodging. We have permitted you to interact with our children. Now, we expect you to honor us by joining in this sacred ritual."

It was a compelling argument. Guntar continued, "If you must know everything, and it seems that you must, we are invoking the spirits of our dead ancestors to come down tonight and give us advice about our problems and concerns. Everyone here must take part or the ancestors will not appear. The dancers, in spite of what you must be thinking, are not drunk. They are possessed by those spirits which we've entreated to join us. The horses allow the dancers to do things that their mere bodies alone could not support. Now, go eat and drink. Pick a horse and dance. Put on a mask first so that the spirits will know that you are one of us and not just a mere human. Set your spirit and emotions free. Be one with the Moon-God."

How could we refuse. We were just a few among many. We would dishonor our hosts if we resisted. The eyes of the Indonesians were on us as we began to rise from our seats on the ground. They followed us as we went to the table and took some leaves and coconut shells. The eyes tracked us as we ate and drank. Their heads nodded in approval as we began to writhe in time to the gamelans' hynnotic music. Their lips seemed to form words of surprise as we mounted our hobby horses and began to trot and gallop. Their mouths gasped in amazement when we fell to the ground, our eyes glazed and arms raise to the Moon-God.

While lying motionless on the ground, I asked their god to let me live through the miseries and deprivations that I knew were yet to come before this journey was finished. I asked for a safe trip back to the kindness and mercy that only our God can provide. But, the Moon-God provided no sign, no promise of mercy, as I lay there on the ground on the island of Java in the country of Indonesia so very far from home and family.

He just shone in arrogant brightness as he mocked my attempts to engage him. I begged. I wept. I made a drunken fool of myself to the delight of the audience. My hobby horse lay broken and immobile between my legs. My mask had fallen off. My tears had turned the ground to mud.

Did this far-off god know me to be a sinner, a hypocrite, an apostate, as my home God surely did? I sensed no forgiveness from this god. He only gloried in his own brightness. He was a vain god. He was full of himself. He mocked me. I realized that night in that far off moon lit jungle that gods are not alike. And, for that, I am glad.

Tonight, many years later, I am lying in my bed in soft comfort. My wife is lying beside me as she has for sixty-five years. I am a lucky man. I know of a better God. I see the full moon through my bedroom window. I have seen him before. I rode a wooden horse while in a drunken stupor as I searched for meaning and forgiveness in a jungle in a land far away.

Stupid moon! Shine your light on the jungle. I have no need for it.

THE AMERICAN TEACHER

Ivan had never met an American. He was more curious than afraid, but he was a little nervous. His grandfather had regaled him about the loud, hard-drinking GI's whom he'd met when the two armies met in Berlin. He said that they loved to brawl and boast about their conquests with the women.

But, this American was a teacher, not a soldier. The class had received a picture of him a few weeks ago. Ivan had studied the face of the pleasant-looking middle aged man to look for signs. His mother had told him to look in his eyes because eyes are the mirrors of a man's soul. He had looked long and hard, but he saw nothing alarming. He hoped for the best. Ivan wanted to learn about America. He yearned to know more about that country where everyone was rich, had many cars, televisions and food from all over the world. He'd heard that most Americans lived in single-family homes that had big yards and a garage for their expensive cars. That was in sharp contrast to the small, grimy apartment where he lived.

He would ask this man how many rooms were in his house. He'd heard that they had as many as seven or eight. He would ask him if he knew any Indians or cowboys. How many guns did he own? Had he every shot anyone or know any gangsters? The old American television shows that he'd seen on his old black and white set had made America look vivid and colorful even on that fuzzy cracked screen.

He'd listened to his parents and their friends rail against capitalism and the inequalities it produced. But, to Ivan, even the poorest Americans seemed to live better than his family and the families of his friends. He hoped that the month that the visiting teacher planned to be with them would be long enough for him learn all the he wanted to know about America and Americans.

The school's principal met the American at the bus station and brought him to the school for a speech before an all-school assembly. Ivan looked at him closely from his front row seat. He thought that he looked tired and a little nervous. After an eight thousand mile trip and not having any sleep for thirty hours, that was not surprising.

The American wore an expensive looking sport coat and contrasting slacks. He had on a light blue button-down shirt open at the neck in the new fashionable style. Ivan liked the way that he smiled at everyone and acknowledged their applause in a shy, modest way.

Ivan thought that he spoke in a strange cadence, somewhat different from how his English instructor spoke. But, he'd heard that American English has a different sound from the British English that was taught in his school. Ivan strained to understand what he was saying. But, he got the gist of it. He said that his name was Mr. Wallace, Jim Wallace. He wanted the students to call him Jim. Ivan's regular teachers insisted on being addressed as "Mr.," "Mrs.," or "Miss." Ivan liked the informality. He decided that he liked Mr. Wallace, also. He would need to get accustomed to calling him Jim.

Later, Ivan found out that Mr. Wallace would be teaching the English class that Ivan was enrolled in. What a lucky break! That night at home, Ivan stayed up late to prepare a list of question that he'd ask Mr. Wallace as the opportunities arose. Just before he got into bed, his parents came in to tell him goodnight. That was unusual. After some awkward conversation, his dad came to his intended point. "Don't get too friendly with this American," he warned. "They can be tricky." His parents had been students during the Second World War and young adults during the so-called cold war. They had been bombarded with anti-American propaganda about the deceitfulness of those uppity Americans. They were so full of themselves and their possessions. "Just watch yourself," they admonished.

The next day, his regular English teacher, Miss Olachik, introduced Mr. Wallace to Ivan's class. The told them that he would be their teacher for the next month. She would be there to help interpret and to provide help when needed. Mr. Wallace would be emphasizing conversational English and idiomatic expressions that Americans called "slang."

The class was excited. This was the first Amerikanski that they'd over met. The girls tittered with embarrassment when he said how pretty they all looked. He liked, especially, their long pigtails. He complimented the boys on their well-groomed appearance and their obvious physicality. He told them that they'd make good American football players.

He told the class the he looked forward to teaching them and getting to know them. He hoped that they would learn more about American and that he would learn more about their great country. He considered himself to be an ambassador, an agent of good will. He knew that the two countries had been at odds over many issues in the past. His goal was to show that the two peoples were very much alike and shared the same dreams and aspirations.

All the while that he talked, Miss Olachik was busy translating his words into Russian. Ivan hoped that she would stay out of the process and let the students try to understand Mr. Wallace without too much help from her. They would learn better that way.

Ivan liked "Jim." He seemed really nice. He was not like the cowboys, gangsters and over-paid athletes depicted on those old American television shows. Take away his expensive clothes, fine watch and ring and he was just like Russian men. Except for their excessive drinking carousing. His dad and most of the Russian men that Ivan knew, loved their vodka and their smelly Russian cigarettes.

More and more, Ivan caught himself comparing Mr. Wallace to the other men in his life. "Jim" knew a lot about literature, music and art. He told the class that emphasis on those things was what separated great societies from the ones that history will forget. He worked a lot of discussion of the arts into his daily English lessons. Most of the Russian men whom Ivan knew, scoffed at such things. When he told his dad that he wanted to be like Mr. Wallace and know more about those things, his dad told him that they were for women and sissies. He became noticeably angry and said, "And furthermore, if you don't stop glorifying this effete American, I'll take you out of his class." Ivan was surprised at his dad's strong reaction.

Ivan knew from his wide reading that Russia had once been the home of many great writers, musicians and artists. He knew, also, that under their current government, art in all forms had been suppressed and those who attempted to use their creativity were punished and, even, exiled. Ivan considered that to be a crime against the human spirit. But, he didn't want to make his dad even angrier. He nodded his head in tacit submission and kept his mouth shut.

In spite of his dad's warning, Ivan and Mr. Wallace became closer. They both seemed to feel a bond. Ivan felt that they had many similar ideas about almost every thing. With just a few day's left in his time in Russia, Mr. Wallace told Ivan that he'd like to meet with his parents if that could be arranged. Ivan was not certain how his parents would react to this request. He remembered his dad's angry outburst about Mr. Wallace's support of the arts.

But, that evening, he mentioned the idea to his parents at the dinner table. Dad laughed at the idea. Mom kep silent as usual. Dad wondered what Mr. Wallace's motivation was. Did he want to see their sad little poorly furnished apartment in the trash littered "bad" part of the city? Did he want to embarrass them? They had only one big room that was partioned off with drapes to provide some privacy for sleeping. They had to share a kitchen and a bathroom with the other three families on their floor. Ivan conceded that he would be ashamed to let Mr. Wallace see how they lived.

Ivan would try to persuade Mr. Wallace to meet with him and his family somewhere else. Maybe, the local cafe.

Dad asked something that Ivan thought was strange when he opened the drape to tell him goodnight. He asked Ivan if he'd noticed anything unusual or odd about Mr. Wallace. Ivan told him that all Americans might seem a little strange to us, but nothing very unusual stood out. Dad just grunted and said, "Well, just keep your eyes open, something is up, that's for sure."

As Ivan drifted off to sleep, he wondered what his dad meant by "strange."

The next morning, Ivan told Mr. Wallace that it might be better not to come to his family's apartment. Mr. Wallace said that he only wanted to see how the average Russian family lived. Ivan felt bad, but he didn't want "Jim" to see the deplorable condition in which he lived. Ivan didn't mention the possiblilty of meeting elsewhere.

The last few days of Mr. Wallace's visit went by quickly. Ivan and his classmates had enjoyed the interchange of information about their country and America. They were amazed at how quickly Mr. Wallace had learned their language, even the subtle nuances. Their use of the Cyrillac alphabet made it even more difficult for most foreigners to learn to speak, write and listen. "Jim" must be very intelligent, they all agreed. After just a month, he's speaking like a native.

The next morning, Mr. Wallace came into Ivan's classroom a little earlier than usual. He was talking on his cell phone. Ivan entered and took his seat. He, usually, came in early, also, to have some extra time with Mr. Wallace before class began. "Jim" moved further away form Ivan and continued to talk, but in a softer voice. Ivan thought that Mr. Wallace was talking in Russian, but couldn't be quite certain. If he is, he thought, that's really remarkable. He must have a rare talent for learning languages.

That night, Ivan told his parents about Mr. Wallace's surprising ability to learn to speak Russian. He not only had learned their language, but acts like an adopted son of Mother Russia. His dad looked concerned. He asked Ivan if Mr. Wallace had been acting nervous or seemed to be on edge. Ivan said that the only thing different lately was that he had been asking a lot more questions about the students' families and their living conditions. But, he was a scholar and a teacher. Those people always have a bigger than normal curiosity about the world and the people in it. Also, he'd been told that Americans, especially, were noted for their curiosity about personal things. He liked that about Mr. Wallace. He wished that his dad and the other men whom he knew would be able to talk more openly about such things. Dad had always said that type of talk is for the women.

Dad warned Ivan not to talk about their income, their possessions or, especially, dad's job. It was none of that nosey American's business. He had no right to try to get information from his students about their home life. It wasn't part of his duties as a teacher, at least not in this country.

Later, just before Ivan fell asleep, dad parted the drapes once again, came into Ivan's sleeping area and sat down on his bed. "Son," he said, "I've been thinking. I don't want you to mention our new car, the Lada, that I keep under the tarp in back of the apartment. I don't want anyone but family and a few friends to know about it. People might want to borrow it and I don't want any of those drunken fools to touch it." With that, he patted Ivan on the head and closed the drape. Well, that was unusual, Ivan thought. He never pats me. It's usually a swat.

Dad had told Ivan when he brought home the new car that he'd won some money in the state lottery. It was their first new car. It wasn't grand, like the big flashy ones that the mafia drove around proudly. But, it made Ivan proud to see it sitting there all wrapped up like a christmas present. Dad hadn't even driven it yet. He said he was waiting for the right time.

Ivan peeked out of his sleeping area. Dad was sitting at the kitchen table drinking his usual nightcap of pivo. He had a worried look on his face. Mom sat across from him looking sad as usual. Even mom was having a pivo.

As dad had warned, Mr. Wallace spent a lot of time durng his last days asking a lot of questions about the students' personal lives. He told the class that he wanted to learn all that he could before returning to America. It was fun for the students to skip their usual lessons and just talk to Mr. Wallace. He described his home, the town he lived in, what he ate and his possessions. They were all envious of the comparative luxuries that he, his family and friends all seemed to have. The students, in turn, opened up about how they and their friends lived. Ivan vowed that, one day, he would visit America and see for himself.

One thing did bother Ivan. Mr. Wallace did seem unusually interested in what the students' parents did for a living. Most of them worked in the factory that made the ubiquitous Ladas that almost everyone drove. It was a small, cheap car with utilitarian styling. They were no match for the cars that Mr. Wallace described. He, even, had shown them a picture of his Cadillac Seville.

When Mr. Wallace asked them how many of their families owned a Lada, most of the students raised their hands. Ivan began to wonder what this question had to do with Mr. Wallace wanting to learn about Russian life. But, maybe "Jim" was a car enthusiast.

That night, Ivan told his dad about Mr. Wallace's curiosity about Ladas. Dad scowled and retreated into his curtained sleeping area. Ivan heard him talking on the telephone in a subdued voice. Dad redialed several times and seemed to be repeating the same conversation. When dad came out from behind the drape, he told Ivan in a commanding voice, "Do not, I repeat, do not, tell Mr. Nosey anything else about our family. Do you understand?" Ivan nodded his head.

The next morning, Miss Olachik was back in front of the class. She deflected questions about the whereabouts of Mr. Wallace. "Don't worry," she said. "You'll find out soon enough." Ivan worried about Mr. Wallace. Was he ill? Was his family ill? Did he need to return home for an emergency? He had hoped to, at least, say goodbye to him. He had neglected to get his mailing address so that they could keep in touch.

Something was wrong. The principal and the teachers seemed anxious and nervous. It carried over to the students. The entire school seemed to be on edge. No one knew why. Or, at least, those who did know, were keeping quiet.

After school, Ivan walked slowly down the six blocks to his apartment complex. It was a cement block building of eight floors. It looked like all of the other Soviet era buildings. It was called Building Number Six. The word "ambiance" was never used in connection with it.

The first things that Ivan noticed were the eight police cars that had formed a ring around the perimeter of the building. Their lights were flashing that eerie police blue. Officers stood by their cars with their hands on their gun belts. Had there been a crime? Had someone been shot, or, worse, killed? Ivan wondered if his parents were safe.

As he neared the south entrance which led up to his apartment, he saw a man whom he thought was Mr. Wallace. But, what would he be doing here? It must be a mistake. The man had on the same type of expensive trench coat and the same stylish leather driving cap. He was talking loudly with an officer who wore the shoulder bars of a captain. He spoke in Russian.

A police officer saw Ivan and told him to move farther away. Ivan told the officer that he lived here and was concerned about his parents. The officer's mood softened and he told Ivan that he could stay if he moved back. Ivan took a position behind a large birch tree. He could still see what was going on and could still hear the conversation between the man who looked like Mr. Wallace and the police captain.

From the bits and pieces of their conversation that he could hear, Ivan could tell that the captain was showing great respect for the other man. It was evident that the Wallace look-a-like was someone of great importance. Ivan didn't know what to think. Were the two men play-acting? Was a movie being shot and his apartment was being used as the location?

Was it really Mr. Wallace? As Ivan continued to look and listen, he learned that several men who lived in the apartment and worked at the Lada factory had formed a black market ring to provide their factory managers with fresh meat, produce, dairy products, wine and vodka - all of the those things that were in high demand and short supply. They were strong-arming local farmers and grocers to give them those products and, in return, they wouldn't beat them up or destroy their farms or stores. The factory managers gave each thug a new Lada for their efforts by falsifying factory shipment and purchase records.

Ivan was glad that voices carried well via the crisp, cold Russian winter air. He sensed that his dad had received their new Lada in this same fashion. As he listened, it became clear that Mr. Wallace had been working undercover in Ivan's school to garner the information needed for conviction. He held a high rank in the intelligence section of the feared KGB. He had wanted to do this himself instead of sending a subordinate. He told the captain that he feared that he was getting rusty sitting behind his desk instead of being out in the field once again. He seemed animated and happy. The captain addressed him several times as Comrade Walatchkiva.

He told the captain that he had studied English at Moscow State University and used that knowledge as a field interpreter in the Red Army's negotiations with the American military after the capture of Berlin in World War Two.

As Ivan continued to watch and listen from behind his tree, his dad and five other men were led out of the apartment building with their wrists in handcuffs and their heads bowed. Ivan hid further from sight. He didn't want his dad to know that he saw his shame. He felt that he had betrayed his dad by trusting "Mr. Wallace."

As the men were placed in the police cars, Comrade Walatchkiva noticed Ivan behind the birch tree. He walked over with a big smile on his face and an outstretched arm. Ivan looked down and didn't return the smile or offer his hand. In perfect English, the comrade told Ivan that he'd been a good student and it had been a pleasure to have been his teacher.

As a last remark before getting into his police model Lada, he said, "I hope that you have learned your lesson well."

ST. PETERSBURG

No, it's not Florida. It's the Soviet Union. And, no, it's not 2015, it's 1972. I'm here as a member of a delegation of the National Association of Secondary School Principals to study the Soviet educational system. We hope to learn some new ideas or, more likely, see some old ones. I flew from Cleveland to New York City where I boarded a Scandinavian Airlne plane for the flight to Helsinki, Finland. I waited three hours in Helsinki to board an Aeroflot jet to St. Petersburg. I met up with the other members of our group at the Leningradskaya Hotel which was located on the bank of the Neva River near the center of the city. I could look across the river at the Fortress of Peter and Paul where many of the Russian czars, including Peter the Great were entombed. Just down the river, lay the enormous Winter Palace which housed the famous Hermitage Museum.

After settling into my small, spartan room, I spent some reflective time staring out of the window at the panorama which lay before me. My fouth floor room gave me a great view of this historic city. It was March and the weather was still very cold. The fur-clad Russians walking along the Neva's embankment created clouds of steam. I was anxious to join those throngs of stalwart Soviet citizens in their daily walks. Personal automobiles were few, so walking and the use of the underground trains were their chief modes of transportation.

I would try very hard to create some personal time between our school visits so that I could experience the city and the lives of its inhabitants. Our group had a very busy itinerary of visits and attendance at cultural events. But, I wanted to see the city on my own terms. I would find a way.

Our visit was during the time of the so-called "Cold War." Tensions were high. The USSR and the United States were blaming each other for the various world problems. The respective virtues and problems of capitalism and communism were discussed and argued ad nauseam. Neither country was willing to admit that any good could come from the other's form of government.

Spyng and expionage were at an all-time high. We had been told in our briefings at the United States Embassy and, to a lesser extent, at the Soviet Embassy, that our hotel rooms were wired for sound and that we would be monitored in our daily activities. We were warned not to visit certain areas, not to talk to certain people and not to photogaph certain thing. There were many "don't' and very few "do's." It promised not to be a typical tourist's vacation.

I continued staring out of my window until darkness settled in. We were as far north as Anchorage Alaska and complete darkness settled in early. That's how it is in the far north during the winter months. By contrast, it never gets completely dark during May, June and July. That period is known as the "White Nights" here in St. Petersburg.

I slept fitfully that first night. I was excited to be here. The city's history, literature, music and architecture had fascinated me ever since I took a college course in Russian history. Now, here I was in the midst of it. Between periods of wakefulness, I dreamt that Peter himself had gotten down from his horse on the pedestal that was near to the Admiralty Building to give me his personal welcome to his namesake city. I accepted graciously on behalf of all of the citizens of my hometown, Mogadore, Ohio. He tempered his greeting by warning me not to misbehave while here and not to underestimate the power and reach of the KGB. My colleagues and I were welcome to visit, but not to meddle, propagandize or disobey the rules of conduct for visitors. Because Peter stood about seven feet tall, I found it difficult to ignore his admonishments. He re-mounted his horse and assumed his heroic pose.

From my readings in preparation for the trip, I had learned that Peter's famous monument was built by the order of Catherine The Great to honor her predecessor. At its base, were the words both in Latin and Russian, "Catherine the Second to Peter the First." Peter's horse is shown stepping on a snake which represented the enemies of Peter and all those who opposed his sweeping reforms. The horse stands on its hind legs and Peter's arm points forward to the future. The statue took twelve years to build. The base is the largest stone ever moved by humans. It weighed over

1500 tons. The statue and pedestal together stands 45 feet tall. Legend has it that as long as "The Bronze Horseman" stands in Senate Square, Russia will remain unconquered by its enemies. It withstood the horrific siege of the city by German forces during World War Two. Thousands of buildings were destroyed, but Peter's statue remained unscathed. During the bombings and shellings, it was covered by sandbags and a wooden shelter.

I don't want to make this into a history lesson, but I was thrilled to be in St. Petersburg amid all of its beauty and history. It's, truly, one of the world's great cities. As background for what happened to me during that visit, following are just a few more facts.

In 1914, St. Petersburg's name was changed to Petrograd in order to be rid of the hated Germanic word "burg." In 1924, the name was changed to Leningrad to honor Vladimir Lenin, the hero of the Bolshevik Revolution. In 1991, the city became St. Petersburg once again.

It is known as the "Revolution City." The revolutions of 1905 and 1917 which precipitated the overthrow of the czars both began here. The cruiser Aurora, which is anchored in the Neva River, fired the shots that began the shelling of the Winter Palace. The ship is now a museum of the revolution.

The bravery of its citizens during the 872 day siege of the city during The Second World War resulted in it being named one of the four Russian "Hero Cities."

The next morning, our group of nine American principals met in the hotel's dining room for breakfast. We had soft-boiled eggs {very soft), slices of ham, cucumber salad in sour cream, limp, soggy toast and very strong coffee. I gave my salad to Father Hugh, a burly parochial school principal from New York City who had played professional football with the Giants. I had, already, picked him out to be a great walking companion.

Our group leader and Olga, our guide from the Friendship House, gave us instructions for the day's activities. Olga was a comely young lady who spoke beautifully precise English. The Friendship House provided guides who specialized in accompanying foreign visitors on sightseeing tours. We had been told that they, also, reported violations of the strict rules that governed such visitors. Rumor had it that they worked for the KGB. I had trouble believing that Olga, who was young, blonde and friendly, was an agent of that ruthless government agency.

I asked some questions about taking pictures and talking to Russian citizens. The answers were: "Don't take pictures of anything that would embarrass The Soviet Union or talk to anyone about politics, the military or religion." The answers were vague enough to keep me still wondering. What is embarrassing? What does politics mean exactly? Is there any difference between philosophy and religion? I resolved to just use my common sense. But, my common sense often differs from the common sense of others.

The first on item on the day's itinerary was a conducted bus tour of the city. I hoped that we would stop long enough at each important site to allow me to take some quality pictures. Photography was high on my list of priorities for the trip. I hoped to do slide shows and write articles when I returned home.

The bus tour lasted four hours. We had many stops. I was able to take many pictures. I began to wonder if I had brought enough film with me. Would 24 rolls of 36 exposures each be enough? I didn't want it to be necessary to buy the poor quality Russian film.

I was admonished by Olga only twice. Once, for trying to snap a picture of an old lady sleeping on a park bench who had all of her worldly possessions in a large shopping bag lying beside her. Another time, Olga grabbed my arm when a Red Army soldier walked by in a full uniform that displayed a full chest of colorful medals. Olga said rather loudly, "No military!"

As the bus moved from place to place, Olga gave us a lecture about the city over the public address system. She was a fount of information. From her, we learned that St. Petesburg was the northern most city in the world with a population of over one million. In fact, five million people lived there. It had 220 museums, 2000 libraries, 80 theaters and 100 concert halls. It was known as the cultural center of the USSR.

As I write this, I see that I've fallen into the trap of calling the country "Russia," when in fact, back when these events took place, it was The Union of Soviet Socialist Republics. Russian was just one of the thirteen republics. Hence, the use of USSR.

During the four hour trip, we managed to see most of the sites that I'd read about in my preparation for the trip. I hoped to get back to some of them on my own time. When we returned to the hotel, I washed up, put more film in my camera bag and took off on my own. Actually, it was not on my own. When I exited the hotel, a big guy in an ill-fitting suit followed close behind me. I realized that it was true, we would be watched closely. I tried to act as if my shadow were not there, but a six foot four, 250 pound shadow is difficult to ignore. I walked along the Neva River embankment past some impressive buildings and tree-laden parks. I entered one of the parks and saw several chess games in progress. Classical music was playing from speakers placed high up in the trees. What a great idea! I stopped at one of the chess games and stood behind the players to watch. My shadow stopped and watched me. I took out my camera, trying to act nonchalant. The big guy didn't move or change expressions what I aimed the camera and snapped a picture. I guess that the chess picture would not be an embarrassment to the Soviet Union.

After about an hour of strolling around, my shadow and I returned to the hotel just in time for my group's scheduled dinner. As we ate, we shared stories of the day's adventures. Our dinner consisted of salad, borscht, boiled beef tongue, mashed potatoes and a small dish of very good ice cream. Two large bottle of wine were placed at each table. We ate the boiled tongue with some trepidation.

I arranged with Father Hugh to take a walk later that evening. We met in the lobby at eight o'clock. As we left the hotel, my shadow followed along behind. Hugh's shadow must have had the night off.

The streets and parks were still crowded. The Neva was full of private and commercial water craft. The full moon cast its light on the water creating a scene worth being painted. Here I was, walking in the moonlight with a very large New York City priest, followed by a very large KGB goon in the beautiful city of St. Petersburg in the very large country of the Soviet Union. What a picture!

We lost track of time. We must have walked four or five miles. The city's entire population seemed to out either walking or sitting on the numerous riverside benches. Sometime during the night, my shadow must have grown tired or decided that we were no threat to is country. We couldn't see him, anyway. Who know if he could still see us. When we returned to the hotel about one o'clock in the morning, we found the lobby doors locked and no one in sight. We knocked politely. No one came. We knocked louder. Finally, a little old cleaning lady came to the door. She looked around to see if her superiors were near and opened the door with a slight smile. I heard her whisper to herself, "Amerikanskis." I handed her an American dollar bill. Her toothless smile became broader.

Hugh and I went to the bank of elavators and rang for our floors. Hugh gave me large priestly bear hug and wished me God-speed. The elevator door opened and an elderly babushka, grandmother, sat inside on a stool and gestured for me to say which floor. I held up four fingers and she pushed the number four button. I could have done that myself, but the Soviet government gave such jobs to the elderly to bolster their meager pensions. Another good idea in a land of mostly bad ideas.

The next day, we visited schools. I and three other principals visited School Number Twenty-five. It was located on a residential street two blocks off of the city's main drage, Nevsky Prospekt. It was a one story cement block building that looked like thousands of other such structures built during Stalin's era. Those buldings were in sharp contrast to the more aestheically pleasing buildings built by French and Italian architects during the reign of Peter The Great. Those original buildings were painted in a variety of pastel colors to liven up the sunless days of this far-northern city. St. Petersburg is referred to often as "The Venice of the North" because of the colorful buildings and its many canals.

The first class that I visited was one of third grade students. The girls wore black dresses with white aprons. Most of the girls had their hair tied back with white bows. The boys wore white long sleeve dress shirts with black ties and black trousers. All of the students arose when I entered the room and said, "Hello, sir!" in perfect English. This was an English specialization school. All classes in all subjects were conducted in English. It was obvious that the students were more advanced than most American students. In addition to English, algebra, geometry, basic chemistry and basic physics were being taught.

The teacher asked if I would mind answering some of the students' questions. The students were very curious about all things American. "Of course not," I answered. Some questions were: "Do you know any Indians?" "Do gangsters live near you?" "Do you own a gun?" "Have you ever killed anyone?" "How many cars do you own?" "How many rooms does your house have?" "How big is your television?" "Do you need to share your kitchen and bathroom with your neighbors?"

Obviously, what they knew about America came from watching old American movies or television re-runs.

I came away from many more such visits with an appreciation for much of the Russian educational system. I learned that Russian students were advanced compared to us in most areas, especially, in mathematics, science and language instruction. Sports, music, and drama were handled by community organizations, not the schools. The schools concentrated on academics. Most schools were in session six days each week for eight hours each day. Vacation time was taken two weeks at a time, interspersed throughout the calendar year, not just in the summer months. Another great idea. That evening, our group was treated to a performance of Swan Lake at the Kirov Ballet Theater. The beautiful music and the dancing served as a soporific for a peaceful night's sleep. Before lying down on my narrow, too short cot, I stood for a while looking out of my room's window at the Neva winding its way through the heart of the city. Across the river, the lights of the Peter and Paul Fortress shone brightly. Inside lay the remains of the mighty czars of this huge self-isolated country. Down the river, the dark outline of the Winter Palace could be seen only faintly. Inside, the treasure and spoils of this once and mighty empire were stored for viewng by generations to come.

I realized how lucky I was to be able to experience the wonders and excitement of this fascinating land. Churchill once described it as being "A riddle wrapped in a mystery inside an enigma." How true that is, but that label is of its own choosing. The czars and the more modern leaders have chosen to be a country apart, a kind of pariah among nations. So, it will be up to me to learn as much as I can on my own. I can't expect much help from within.

As I continued to look out of my window, a snow white pidgeon flew out of the darkness and landed on the window sill. I chose to consider that as being an omen. An omen that would bring me and my fellow travelers good fortune while here and safe passage home.

During our month-long stay, we visited many more interesting sites and many more schools. We ate a lot of borscht and sour cream, chicken Kiev and blinis, a kind of pancake. We were introduced to kvass, a grain alcohol made from fermented rye bread. The drink was sold on street corners from small tanks on wheels. We drank soft drinks from dispensers placed throughout the city. Just one glass was provided for all who bought from them. The delicious Russian ice cream was sold by street vendors both in summer and winter. We were told that if it were too sweet, it meant that extra sugar had been used to cover up the taste of souring milk and cream.

We became accustomed to the long hours of darkness and the surveillance of the ever-present government watch dogs. We learned to take pictures when not looking like we were taking pictures. We learned that Russian drivers usually ignore stop signs and pedestrian cross-walks. We never did learn how to navigate the marvelous subway system with its multi-level tracks and signs in the Cyrillic alphabet.

Olga continued to be our source of information about all things St. Petersburg which, by the way, the locals referred to as simply "Pete." It's like calling St. Louis, "Louie."

Near the end of our stay, Olga took me aside and said that she'd like to show me some of the beautiful underground subway stations. She said that they were adorned with murals, crystal chandeliers and marble statuary. So, that afternoon, we walked to the nearest station, Avlovo, some four blocks from the hotel. Nearing the station, I stepped off of the curb without looking both ways. Before a speeding car could hit me, Olga grabbed my arm and pulled me back to the curb. I tried to thank her by giving her an impulsive hug, but she pushed me back roughly and said, "I am not a cat to be stroked. We don't show affection in public." I felt embarrassed and little surprised. She had been very open and friendly in all of our dealings. But, point well taken. I learned, also, that Russian drivers show little regard for pedestrians, especially, foreign ones.

When we entered the station, I was shocked by its gaudy opulence. It looked like a palace. I couldn't help but to compare it to the New York City and London underground stations. We took a train to the next station. It was equally lavish. The trains ran on three levels that were reached by very steep escalators, some of which were more than 300 feet below ground level. After we rode several more trains to sample more stations, we returned to the hotel. On the way back, I sensed that Olga had wanted to talk about more than the city's underground system. I was very correct.

As we neared the hotel, she stopped, took my arm, and asked me if I'd like to visit with her and her roommates in the privacy of their dormitory room. I was surprised and a little concerned. Olga lived in the women's dormitory of the St. Petersburg State University where she was studying English literature. She was a senior and would be graduating in a few months. What if I were being set up? Would going there be in violation of university rules? Would I be violating my rules of conduct for foreign visitors? What if I were arrested and my visa were revoked? What if I had to stay in the USSR until the investigations and the trial were concluded? I thought over a lot of "What if's" before I said, "I'd like that."

The visit would give me an opportunity to see how students lived and, more importantly, what they thought. We arranged for me to accompany her to the university the next day after our group's activities were finished.

The next day passed quickly with visits to St. Isaac's Cathedral and the Pushkin Theater. At four o'clock, Olga met me in the lobby and we walked across the bridge over the Neva to the state university. It was located on a sprawling campus near the Fortress of Peter and Paul. We entered the front door of the dormitory building and stopped at the guard's desk. The corpulant middle-aged woman dressed in a military uniform looked me up and down and gave Olga a questionning look. Olga said something in Russian. I picked out the words "American," "educator," and "friend." That seemed to mollify the guard enough to continue speaking to Olga in a less severe tone. Later, Olga told me that the guard said that I'd need to meet the students in a group, not individually, and that I would need to be out of the building by eight o'clock this evening. No later.

I followed Olga down the hall to the elavators where we rode up to the fourth floor. We walked down a long dimly lit corridor to room number eleven. Actually, it was not a room, but a small suite containing a sitting room, two bedrooms and a bathroom. Three female students sat in the living room awaiting our arrival. On the table in front of the sofa, bread, butter, assorted jams and a coffee service were displayed. I was invited to sit down and help myself to the food and drink. All of this talk was in English that had a decidedly British accent.

After some moments of awkward attempts to create small talk, The four girls began to ask me questions about my life in America. In return, I countered with questions about their lives. We discussed the relative merits of Lenin, Lincoln, Stalin, Roosevelt, Rasputin, Burr, Dostoyevski, Whitman, Rachmaninov, Gershwin, and many other notable figures from both countries. I think that we learned a lot and were able to correct many false impressions. I saw Olga glancing at her watch several times. At about 7:30, Olga told the other three young ladies that I would need to leave soon and that she would accompany me to the lobby. I said my goodbyes and Olga and I left the suite.

We walked past the grim-faced guard who wrote down something on her ledger. Olga surprised me by continuing to walk with me until we reached the end of the university grounds near the river. Olga motioned for me to sit down with her on a wooden bench which overlooked the dark waters of the Neva. She looked back toward the dormitory and, when convinced that no one had followed us, leaned in towards me and began talking in a quiet voice.

"I hope that you have enjoyed your visit in our country. I have noticed that you seem very interested in our culture, our music, our literature and our way of life in general. You've made many nice comments about our schools and how advanced they are compared to yours. I overheard you say to one of your fellow educators that you wouldn't mind living here for a while if you could persuade your wife to move here with you."

I listened to Olga in surprise. Had I given her and her superiors the wrong impression? I had just made some off-the-cuff comments about the things that I'd experienced. I really had no desire to stay longer, let alone live here, even for a short time. I was just joking when I said I'd like to move here. There was no way that I'd really do it.

Olga continued: "Even if you don't arrange to live here for a while, you could be a big help to both of our countries if we could arrange to continue communicating with each other when you return home. My superiors could set that up for us. From time to time, you could let me know how you and your friends are doing and what the climate of your country seems to be in regard to relations with our country. We just want some verifiable news about your economy, morale and world views in general. Doing that shouldn't cause you any trouble. What do you think?"

What I thought was that I was being recruited to be a spy for the USSR. Olga had made it sound very innocent, but I wasn't naive. I knew how this could escalate and how I could be blackmailed once I'd begun to submit information to Olga and her superiors. Olga sensed my uneasiness and reached over, patted my thigh and smiled. Phew! I liked a little adventure and some intrigue, but it was time for me to leave.

I muttered something about needing to get back to the hotel and got up from the bench. Olga looked at me with an unformed question on her lips. I thanked her for her hospitality and the chance to meet her friends and said that I'd see her at the hotel in the morning for our next adventure.

But, Olga was persistant. She walked with me to the edge of the bridge. As I turned to tell her goodby again, she leaned in and planted a chaste little kiss on my forehead. And, this from the same Olga who had been very clear about displays of affection in public. She whispered, "I'll need an answer very soon."

That night, while standing before my window, looking across the Neva towards the university, I made my decision. I would give Olga a firm "no!" So, this was how spies and double agents are recruited. Why was I singled out? Why not ask one of the other visiting school principals? This unwanted attention made me even more anxious to return home. I had read enough spy thrillers and suffered enough cold-war paranoia to know that even an innocent little kiss on the forehead could lead to some very serious consequences. What if all of this evening's events had been filmed and recorded? I spent a restless night tossing, turning and thinking.

The next morning, a new guide showed up. I never saw Olga again. Many times during the intervening years, I've wondered about her. Did she break with protocol by trying to recruit me? Had her superiors lost their trust in her? Did she over-step her authority by posing as my would-be handler? Was her name really Olga? Was she really just a guide from The House of Friendship? Maybe, she worked for our CIA and was testing my loyalty. After all, I had shown great interest in life here in the USSR.

Maybe, maybe, maybe and maybe.

I do know that my next four trips to the land of czars and borscht included special interviews and searches at the points of entrance and exit. Those next trips covered a span of over twenty years and allowed me to see and experience the great changes that took place in the land that we can call Russia once again.

I do know that each time that I traveled overseas to any foreign country that I underwent special searches and interrogations. I do know that my mail to and from Russia was opened and read by order of our government before it reached my home.

I have rather enjoyed my reputation as a possible intenational spy. The name "Olga" has become for me a metaphor for espionage and intrigue. Sometimes, I wonder what would have happened had I accepted her proposal. Deception has always come easily for me.

My name is Bon------, I mean Smith, Donald Smith

Printed in the United States
By Bookmasters